People Leaving

People Leaving

-stories-

Ian Roy

BuschekBooks

National Library of Canada Cataloguing in Publication Data

Roy, Ian, 1972-
    People Leaving : stories

ISBN 1-894543-06-8

    I. Title.
PS8585.O89835P46 2001   C813'.6   C2001-902266-2
PR9199.3.R65P46 2001

Cover Art: Untitled painting by Jon Claytor (6 x 8 inches), acrylic and pencil on masonite.

The Jean Vanier quote (page 8) is from *Becoming Human* by Jean Vanier (Toronto: House of Anansi) 1998 and is used with the permission of the publisher.

The Sherwood Anderson quote (page 23) is from *Selected Letters: Sherwood Anderson* (Knoxville: The University of Tennessee Press) 1984 and is used with the permission of the publisher.

Second Printing 2006

Printed in Canada by Hignell Book Printing, Winnipeg, Manitoba.

BuschekBooks gratefully acknowledges the support of
the Canada Council for the Arts and the Ontario
Arts Council for its publishing program.

BuschekBooks
P.O. Box 74053, 5 Beechwwod Avenue
Ottawa, Ontario K1M 2H9
Canada
Email: contact@buschekbooks.com
Editor: John Buschek

ONTARIO ARTS COUNCIL
CONSEIL DES ARTS DE L'ONTARIO

The Canada Council | Le Conseil des Arts
for the Arts | du Canada

For Sarah

Loneliness is part of being human, because there is nothing in existence that can completely fulfill the needs of the human heart.

Jean Vanier

Contents

Acknowledgements

I am pleased to acknowledge the City of Ottawa and the Ontario Arts Council for the grants they so kindly provided. For reading earlier versions of these stories and offering advice, criticism, support and inspiration, I would like to thank: Jon Claytor, Mike Feuerstack, Greg Gilbert, and Sharan Samagh. I wish also to express many thanks to my mother, Sherrill Roy, for helping out with Max; John Buschek, for taking this project on; Rita Donovan, for making the editing process so painless; and both the Roy and Caspi families, for the encouragement and love they have shown during the writing of this book. And finally, I would especially like to thank Sarah and Max—for everything.

The story "Choose the Woman" was first published in Geist Magazine.

DANCING

*H*e was an older guy, maybe in his late sixties or early seventies, and he smelled like Old Spice, which is what my father wore when he was alive. Those were the first things I noticed about him: his age and the way he smelled. That says something about me, too, I suppose. He was just like any other old guy you'd see alone in a bar. He was tall and scrawny; gaunt, I guess you'd call him. His face was pock-marked from acne suffered years ago, and his cheeks were sunken under sharp, protruding cheek bones. He had these dark and slightly swollen eyes, sad and moist like a dog's. He looked like a skeleton in a suit. He wasn't bald, though, he still had a full head of hair. It was greased back and dirty gray, but it was all there. It's true, he didn't look great. Not really. But there was something about him that was gentle, and kind of sad. And I guess that's why I let him whisper those things in my ear.

It was supposed to be a Christmas party. But with my husband, Geoff, and his buddies organizing it, it turned out to be just another night out at their regular haunting ground, The Crossroads Bar and Grill. It was really just an excuse for the guys to go out drinking, and for us women to get together before things got too hectic with the holidays. We left the kids with a sitter and drove over after work. After we finished our meal, Geoff and Pete and Hugh sat at the bar for the rest of the night, drinking and smoking and talking. Geoff's not a big drinker like the other two. He just sat between them, sipping his beer and nodding his head every now and then. Pete and Hugh were already drunk before they got from our table to their bar stools. In fact, they were drunk before we even got to the Crossroads. But they're good drinkers; they don't get belligerent and loud like some people I know. Anyway, I sat at the table with their wives, Shirley and Tanya. We drank beer, too, and laughed and complained. We talked about this and about that. The same things we always talk about when we get together: our husbands and kids, work and money.

Shirley had been going on about how hard she tried to keep Pete at home, to help with the kids, to keep her company. She reads all the books, all the magazines and they all tell her the same thing: whether or not it's her fault, it is her responsibility to bring that man back home to where he belongs. Is it a matter of sex? Then give him more sex, or better sex, or less sex, the magazines say. Or maybe it's the stress of work and family, of making ends meet. Then give him scheduled breaks, the books say, a night out with the guys. Make him happy at whatever cost. But work for it; let him know you're his woman, and that his home is there with you. Blah blah blah. I can't believe she buys that crap.

Tanya is the complete opposite. She makes the rules and she does whatever the hell she wants. And it's Hugh who's at home, cleaning up, taking the kids wherever they want to go. I don't mean to say she's a tramp or anything like that, because she's not. She just likes to go out and have fun. She plays bingo obsessively; always has a bingo marker in her purse. I'd say that's where she spends the majority of her time. We tease her, call her a gambling addict. But she says it's not like gambling in a casino—because you see, she's against gambling on principle or for religious reasons or whatever.

In casinos, that is. But the bingo's different, she tells us, the bingo's just for fun. Tanya's funny that way.

Somehow these two women manage to be best friends. And me? I sit there between them, quietly listening, and nodding my head just like Geoff does with their husbands. Geoff and I are somewhere in the middle of the others. We both do the work around the house, we're both home-bodies and Geoff is a wonderful father to the kids. I swear if they were forced to pick a favourite, they'd probably pick him. So we're good; things are fine. I mean, they're good enough, I suppose. I should mention at this point that every once in a while I do think about what it would be like to be on my own again. It's not that I don't love Geoff, I really do. And of course I love the kids more than anything. I suppose it's just—well, boredom. It's no big deal; I'm not miserable. It's the usual: high school sweethearts, been married going on twenty years and so, by now, it has become pretty routine. I'm happy enough, content as can be expected. And I do love him. It's just things aren't what they used to be and so, I don't know if it's because of that, but when that old man came along, well, I didn't think twice about getting up and dancing with him.

Shirley said afterwards that she had not danced with any other man since she and Pete were married. "Well, good for you," I said— not sure whether this was something she was proud of or not. Poor soul, I thought to myself later, there she is, home alone with the kids most of the time, while Pete—I've heard things about Pete— while Pete is out doing whatever it is Pete does. She's never wavered, I can say that much for her. And she's got a good heart. They've all got good hearts—Shirley and Tanya, and even Pete and Hugh.

Anyway, I sat there for a long time wanting to dance but just waiting, and drinking enough beer to get me out there on the floor. That's when the old guy came up to our table. He was no dreamboat, but he had this nice, shy smile that I've always fallen for in a guy. He was wearing this old wrinkled suit, maybe from the Sixties, with thin lapels and a thin tie. It was blue, with pin-stripes. Everything about him was skinny, and not so much attractive as unhealthy looking. But he was very polite, and he spoke so quietly I had to ask him several times what it was he was saying.

"Sorry for intruding, ladies." He cleared his throat and then addressed me specifically. "Would you care to dance, my dear?"

Normally, I can't stand it when someone I don't know calls me dear, but this time it didn't bother me. I let it pass. Shirley and Tanya were almost in hysterics. They thought one of the husbands put him up to it. I glanced over at the guys. They still had their backs to us, drinking and talking and eating salted peanuts.

"Sure," I said. "Sure, I'd like that very much."

Shirley and Tanya thought I was joking, thought I just had to be pulling his leg or something. I mean, the guy was old enough to be my father. But I just wanted to dance and he was so sweet. So he escorted me out to the dance floor. And then he wrapped his long, skinny arms around me tight, like he'd never let go. It was like dancing with a paper cut-out, the way he glided around the floor. He was amazing. Not once did he step on my toes. Not like Geoff who can't dance at all. It doesn't help that he doesn't like dancing, but still he couldn't dance to save his life.

We danced in silence for a while, the old man and me. And when the song ended he didn't loosen his grip but waited, still dancing a little, swaying from side to side in anticipation of the next song. For a skinny guy, he sure could hold on. In the quiet between those first songs, he turned so as to look me in the eyes.

"Are you here *alone?*" he asked.

He said it kind of funny, tilting his head to the side a little— *alone*—like you knew he meant was I there with a man or just with the girls.

"No," I said. "I'm here with my husband."

He loosened up his arms and asked me to point Geoff out to him. And when I did—Geoff and Hugh and Pete were turned in their seats now, watching us—the old guy grinned and waved at him.

"She's a great gal," he said. "You've got a great gal here."

I thought this was the funniest thing I'd ever heard. I may have even blushed. Geoff kind of smiled and waved—I don't know if he even heard what the old guy said. I'm sure he didn't think twice about me dancing with some old man. I mean, he probably thought it was my grandfather I was dancing with out there. Thought I was doing my good deed for the day. Had it been a young stud, some handsome and tanned body builder, well, that might have ruffled his feathers a little, might have brought a little gruffness to his voice. Just enough to let his buddies know who's boss, no real harm. But if he heard what the old guy whispered into my ear after that, well, I can't say one way or the other what he would have done. Probably nothing. He'd say something like, "You're a big girl." or "You can take care of yourself." But then quietly, secretly he'd be upset. I know him, I know what he's like. And I should after twenty years of marriage. But something like this—well, Geoff's not always predictable.

So I didn't tell Geoff what the old man said or about any of it. Not the whole story anyway. And I guess it's always been that way with me and the men in my life; they never hear the whole story. It started with my mom. If I brought home a pair of shoes or a new dress, it was always, "Don't tell your father how much you paid for that." Or that time I brought the stray cat in. My mom told me not to tell my father about that either, and to keep the cat in my closet. The poor thing must have lived in my closet for a month before I finally asked my father if I could keep it. And when I did finally ask, he didn't seem to mind; he said he already knew it was there, that he could smell it. So I grew up thinking that this was a game women played with men, something we're supposed to play out. And it's the same with Geoff. Oh, I tell him things like what a new pair of shoes cost, or where I've been. But other things, the not-so-little things he just doesn't need to know. I keep all that a secret.

A couple of years ago I thought about leaving Geoff and the kids. I met this guy who was crazy about me. Sam was funny and smart and gorgeous. And rich, too. And unlike some guys like that, he was the genuine article. We talked about real things; and he was interested in what I had to say about life and politics and what was going on in the world, or just in my head. We even went out a couple of times—on the sly. It's not like Geoff and I don't talk or go out but it was different with Sam. It was so exciting. And even thinking about it now, I get goose-pimples the way I did when I'd first see him walking towards me in a crowded room. But nothing ever happened between us, nothing like *that*. When it came right down to it, I knew I couldn't walk out on my family. They need me, and I realised that I need them in the same way. I told Sam there was no future for us, nothing could ever happen between us. He said he understood and that he'd have a hard time with the idea of breaking up a marriage anyway. I almost fell for him again right there because I thought that was such a sweet thing to say.

Before long he married some childhood sweetheart he hadn't seen in fifteen years. She just turned up one day and off they went to the chapel. We keep in touch; he's got a little girl now and another baby on the way.

Anyway, Geoff doesn't know how close he came to losing me then. I didn't tell him a thing about it. I didn't see any point in it. I'm sure he noticed I was a little melancholy afterwards, less responsive. But it passed and things returned to how they had once been; nothing really changed after that. It would have torn Geoff apart to know about it. I guess I'm just protective. What happens

though, is that I'm stuck with all of this: the old man, and what he
said. It's all mine and I can't talk to Geoff about it. And I just have
to get it out. I've just got to talk it out to make sense of it.

So we danced for a long time. And he held me tight, the way
you would with someone you've known for a very, very long time.
And I thought, this is okay. Kind of nice, actually, as long as he
keeps his hands off my ass. By that time, Geoff and Hugh and Pete,
and Shirley and Tanya had all forgotten about us there on the dance
floor. They'd all turned away, into their drinks and their boring conversations. Then the old man did this thing. He kind of leaned into
my ear, almost hanging off my neck with his skinny little arms, and
he started whispering so quietly I could barely make out the
words.

"You're a beautiful woman," he said. "You've got a great physique."

Now, even Geoff refers to me as a girl most of the time, so it
was kind of cute to hear this old man call me a woman—and something in the way he said it made it sound like a sexy thing to be.
And that thing about my *physique*, well, I'm not exactly sure what
he meant by that, but seeing as I'm not getting any younger, I just
smiled. But then his voice heated up, like his breath and the words
coming out were hot oil seeping into my ear. And he said things
I've never even heard from my own husband. I listened for a while
because I couldn't believe it. It sounded like I had just dialed a
number from the back of a dirty magazine.

I pushed him away, and he gave me this sheepish smile.

"Do you realize you're talking to someone's mother like that?"

I had used that line before when guys whistled at me in the
street. And it usually worked. But he just laughed and acted like
there was nothing wrong, like he didn't know what I was talking
about. And so I had to laugh, too, like it really was no big deal. And
then he pulled me back in to continue the dance; not rough but he

just kind of stepped into me and hung on. And before long, he was at it again with the talking.

The funny thing is—the embarrassing thing about all this is that I can't say I hated it. I mean, I stayed there with him a long time, just dancing and listening. At first, I felt like pushing and pulling simultaneously. But I stayed there listening to the old man, allowing him to say all those things to me. And okay, after a while, I kind of liked it. But I'm not a pervert. Don't get me wrong. It's not like I went home with him or anything. It's not like I let him feel me up or down or whatever. It felt like I was doing him a favour. He said shocking things. God only knows where he learned to talk like that. I know I've never heard such things before in my life and probably never will again. It was definitely a one-time thing. Thrilling, I guess you'd say, but not something I'd get in the habit of doing.

It's odd, though, because I do feel a little guilty. Almost like I did sleep with him or let him touch me. But I didn't. And he was a perfect gentleman—I mean, he was otherwise a perfect gentleman. After dancing for a long time, he simply loosened his grip, bowed and thanked me for dancing with him. And then he walked away. I stood alone on the dance floor watching him go. And I didn't feel sad or angry or appalled or anything. I just stood there and watched him go. I know I made him happy. He's probably just a lonely old guy. His wife's probably dead and his family's long gone. And he just needed to talk to someone. So I was helping him. Doing a good deed. And that makes it okay. It does. I'm sure it does.

CHOOSE THE WOMAN

I'm trying again… A man has to begin over and over.
Sherwood Anderson

My father converted the old tool-shed in the backyard of our rented suburban home into what he insisted on calling his study. He bought an old wooden desk and a chair with one bad leg at a garage sale. He eventually fixed the chair with duct tape, wrapping a strip around the leg periodically to strengthen it. By the end of the summer, the taped up leg of the chair was as thick as my own twelve-year-old leg. From the house my father brought out a lamp, a typewriter and an extension cord. The only other things kept in there were an old bent shovel, the lawn mower and my bicycle. The shed—or study—had a dirt floor that became muddy when it rained. I still remember mud tracks across the kitchen floor in rainy weather, when my father would come into the house for another cup of coffee. He said he liked writing in there during storms best of all because of the sound the rain made when it hit the tin roof. He spent long hours in his study that summer. When he was not at work doing whatever it was he did at the time—technical writer, courier, bookstore clerk, gas station attendant (he was all of these at one time or another)—he was out in his study, writing and smoking and drinking cup after cup of coffee. He was willing to give up everything else to be a writer; and he eventually did.

He and Mom had troubles from the beginning, even before I was born, but they plodded on and on. Then both of them got too tired, and then he left. But before that, they tried. When I was five or six, they left my sister, Tina, and me with my mother's sister in Halifax—so we would not miss any school—and headed west in an old pickup truck. Across this great land of ours, they had said. They needed a break from the 'daily grind'; needed, they said—their words filtered down to me, a boy of five or six—to recapture the passion of the old days. I overheard my uncle say to my aunt, "This drive'll either make it or break it for 'em." But it did neither.

They were gone for sometime—months, maybe a year. I attended school, read postcards, dreamed of Mom and Dad and Tina and me in some big American car. A happy family on the road. Travelling west on a postcard perfect highway in the desert of Arizona. Or the Rockies. I had no sense of geography other than where the wheels of their truck could take them. Borders crumbled; dividing lines between provinces, states and countries meant nothing to my small hand tracing lines on a map.

They returned but nothing had changed. Dad kept writing. He even sold a couple of stories and articles. Mom kept moving from job to job. Even then, Tina and I only lived with them on and off, depending where the jobs were. They did not want to disrupt our education, they told us; they wanted to live as a happy family someday. It was noble. It never worked, however. It never panned out, as Dad always said. He had a real fondness for Yukon history, though it was one place he had never been.

A few years later they left again. They somehow ended up in Grand Junction, Colorado, with a dog: a happy family at last. Dad wrote during the day and pumped gas at a gas station at night. The station was across the street from a firing range. It made for some good stories, he said. Mom worked as a waitress at a restaurant in town. Dad liked this time in his life, he had things and people to write about. The place was rich with stories, he wrote in one letter. Mom was not so happy. She missed Tina and me but she did have the dog. Then the dog was run over by some kid driving his parents' car. He confessed in the restaurant the following day. He made a big scene, crying and repeating *sorry, sorry, sorry* over and over again. Mom straightened him out and sent him on his way. Champ. The dog's name was Champ. Poor Champ.

After losing Champ, Mom decided it was time to go home. "Luck," she said, "just isn't on my side." She was misquoting an old song she never liked. Dad decided to stay in Colorado and keep working.

Mom flew to Nova Scotia and picked us up. She borrowed some money from my aunt and uncle so we could move back to Ottawa to live with my grandparents. "Sure, people will talk but they don't know. They don't know what's really going on," Mom said. Neither did I, but I did not ask any questions. I was just happy to be with her again. She came and went. "Wherever the jobs are," she explained, "that's where I'll go." She spent most of her time with us, living in her parents' house once again. They lived in the suburbs, on a quiet street where everyone knew one another. It drove Mom crazy that the neighbours knew what had happened between her and Dad. My grandmother denied telling any of them, but they had found out somehow. We tried to live a normal life back then; we hardly ever spoke about Dad. On Saturdays we went out for breakfast and then to a matinee. During the week, Tina and I went to school and Mom worked. We returned home from school before her and watched TV with our grandfather, a habit that had been forbidden when we lived with Dad. We watched TV and ate Kraft Dinner and hot dogs, canned beans and white bread. It was a whole new world for us.

Dad started writing to us again. I figured out that he had met another woman. She was a nurse at a small clinic in Grand Junction.

She filled up once a week at the gas station Dad worked at. They were not in love, Dad said, they just had a lot in common. Mom cried as she told us this. Then she said that she did not care and good for him and other things like that. On some nights I could hear her crying in the room next to mine. And I would pretend to be asleep when she came in to check on me.

— • —

"I am coming home," a postcard warned us. "Will you be there?" Dad drove back in the same old pickup; it was a little more beat up and so was he. His hair was greying at the sides and he weighed ten or twenty pounds more than he did the last time we saw him. Mom welcomed him back with a slap on the wrist. There was crying and sobbing, apologizing and, finally, forgiveness. We moved around often, the four of us. And then something else came up. Things just kept coming up.

Watching them was like watching a tennis match. Eventually both opponents, if equally matched, will simply tire and then it is a matter of time before one misses. And then you have a winner and you have a loser. In this case, you had four losers.

Dad wanted to write. Boy, did he. And Mom? Well, Mom wanted more from life than a series of low paying jobs and a restless husband. They both had decisions to make, choices to make. Dad chose writing. It was his passion. It made him tick, he explained, it kept him going. "I love you all," he told us, "but I just have to do this. I have to try and do this." We were living in the house in the suburbs with the study in the yard when Dad moved out, again, and got his own place. After that, I guess he wrote.

Dad took us out occasionally, Tina and me. Sometimes it would only be me. Tina was at an age where she preferred the company of her friends over that of her father and younger brother. We would walk around town and he would tell me what he was working on. He never shared too many details about his work; he did not want to ruin it by telling the story before he 'told the story'. He was not writing as much as he wanted to in those days: "Just not enough time." And time, he told me, was the one thing he really needed, was what he really wanted. He had a collection of all the rejection notices he had ever received from various magazines and publishers: Sorry, no thank you.

"Sometimes," he said, "what you thought was real gold turned out to be fool's gold."

He told me, too, on one of those visits, that if you have to choose between your passion—what gets you out of bed mornings—and a woman, choose the woman. Only she'll make you happy. The other will starve you.

Another thing Dad always said was, "Do as I say not as I do."

After a while, Dad moved on again. He traded the truck in for a small car and hit the road. We did not hear from him for some-time after this. And then it was a postcard from Winnipeg. Later, it was Calgary. Vancouver. And then back to Winnipeg. A postcard offers more picture than anything else, after the stamp and address there is not much room for writing. And it seemed Dad had less and less to say. He quit writing, he told us in a short postcard, because it just wasn't worth it anymore. In 1987, Dad passed on, as my grand-mother said. He killed himself.

He called just days before and told us he loved and missed us all very much. He even said he had plans to visit in the spring. It had been a long, cold winter for him. He hinted, too, that he had been having 'difficulties', but wouldn't elaborate. Things would get better, he said, they had to get better. He then kissed the phone and said good-bye.

— • —

I was recently talking about my father with his sister, my aunt. She let slip a family secret which she thought I already knew.

"The sickness," she said. "The sickness got him, too."

"Too?" I asked.

"Surely, your father told you about your grandfather."

"I must have forgotten," I lied.

My father never spoke about either of his parents. Tina and I often joked that he did not have any parents. He simply sprung from the head of Zeus is what Tina always said. What I learned was that my grandfather had shot himself in a hunting cabin in Northern Quebec. For awhile, it was said that he was cleaning the gun when it went off. A week later they found the note he had hidden in his underwear drawer. He had been unhappy for a long time, my aunt told me. He had money problems and drinking problems and women problems.

"He had them all," she said, "and he couldn't cope any longer. Your dad was just eleven when it happened. It took him a long time to get over it."

My dad withdrew and stopped speaking for over a month. They had to take him out of school because the teacher wouldn't put up with it any more. Instead of speaking, he began to write long, fantastic stories about imagined people and places. He shared the stories with his sister, but no one else. Not for a long time. But then his silence ended just as abruptly as it had begun, and he continued to speak as if he had been doing so all along. Though he never mentioned his father or what had happened or any of it.

— • —

So many years and miles later, I lie awake, unable to close my eyes to these memories of my father or to that time so long ago. My head, too full of these and other thoughts. Thoughts about decisions I have made, and mistakes—the other things that have made me who I am. And I wonder if he spent sleepless nights, like this, wishing he hadn't made some of the choices he had made, the mistakes that ultimately made him who he was. Wishing, maybe, that he had chosen the woman instead, or his writing, or really, anything else at all.

GOD LOVES A BROKEN HEART

Claudia suspected it for a long time but for some reason which she couldn't explain—would never want to explain—she hadn't done anything about it other than to ask him if something was going on, never specifying what that *something* might be. And when he said no, there was nothing going on—he had not been particularly convincing; he hadn't even asked for clarification of *what* she was referring to—Claudia dropped it. Or pretended to. That was two months ago. It wasn't that she didn't care, or that she was scared of what she'd find out if she persisted, she just wanted him to admit it, to come clean on his own without her having to pry it out of him. The *him* being her husband, Barry, and the *it* being him sleeping with another woman.

It's not that easy, Claudia would think to herself some mornings. *It's just not that simple.* But then her fortieth birthday rolled around and she felt like it *was* that simple; there was nothing left to lose. She wasn't too crazy about birthdays to begin with—and turning forty only seemed to make matters worse.

Ten years ago, a now ex-boyfriend of Claudia's tried to throw her a surprise birthday party. Claudia pulled up to his place and noticed all the cars parked outside; cars belonging to friends and family. She left the motor running and peeked in the window of his house. Inside, all the guests stood under a canopy of brightly coloured streamers and balloons; they all had drinks and noise-makers in hand. And it was all just a little too precious, a little too much. So she got back in her car and drove to an all night diner. She must have sat there for three or four hours, reading the paper, drinking coffee and smoking cigarettes. She didn't want to go home where she knew she would be found, dragged back to the party. She had always been a bit of a loner, a bit of a *freak* according to the boyfriend. The next day, when she answered her phone, the boyfriend said, "Thirty is not old, Claudia. Forty is not even old. Don't take it so hard." But it wasn't only that. It was that. But not only that.

Her fortieth birthday, Claudia predicted, would be the worst by far.

— • —

She looked young for forty; people were always saying she looked great for her age. Some would say she looked young for a thirty year old, or at least a thirty-five year old. The boys at the check-out counter at the supermarket, for instance, the ones who flirted with all the *old* ladies, didn't believe it when Claudia told them her age. *Gigolos*, she called them. But she didn't feel young. She felt old old old. She had recently resorted to hiding the incoming gray hairs on her head by attempting to match the outgoing brown with hair dye. But it made her hair look mousy—the word 'mousy' alone was enough to send her over the edge. She was still tall and slim, and more or less beautiful. But now she was forty. On good days, she accused herself of overreacting about her age, of caring too much. *For God's sake, it's not like turning fifty.* But then she'd be reminded that there are grandmothers in their forties. She'd look at teenage girls and think only of how she could be their mother, not of how she had once been one of them, the way she used to think with an if-I-knew-then-what-I-know-now smile. The months and years slid by underfoot.

Somewhere along the way Claudia and Barry decided not to have any children. *Thank heavens for small miracles,* she thinks in one of her more lucid moments. It's the kind of thing her mother would say if she knew what was going on. Barry didn't want any kids—didn't want anymore, that is. He had two boys from a previous marriage. (Barry had celebrated his fiftieth birthday a few years ago.) He saw the boys once in awhile. They were teenagers now. Big boys, interested in hockey and girls. Really, when it came right down to it, Claudia didn't care too much for the boys. Barry Jr. and Tom. Tom and Jerry, that's what Claudia called them. They lived with their mother in a nice big house in a nice big neighbourhood. Good for them.

The thing was, Claudia knew what kind of guy Barry was when she married him. After all, he had been married to Joanne when they met. Married, to be quite honest, when Claudia and Barry first slept together. But she somehow thought that because it was love, all *for* love, his infidelity could be excused, forgiven, forgotten. Like a simple mathematical equation: Adultery+Love=Immunity. Or something like that.

Some of the facts: Barry was married when Claudia met him, slept with him, and started living with him. To be fair, the divorce was imminent when the co-habitation began. Fact: his wife, Joanne, warned Claudia. "It happened before. It'll happen again!" Sure, sure, Claudia thought, not believing a word of it.

But for the last while Claudia suspected something was going on. Barry had been honest-seeming until then. If he stayed out late, he always had an excuse that Claudia believed— had to believe— and it was usually work-related. But now he barely tried to cover up the fact that he had been out with someone else. He began to smell a little different, to look and speak like a different man. And he started hunting! Although he rarely brought home any game. He said he did it more for the sport of it, for the chance to get out with some of the guys from work, and some of his clients. ("It's like a business trip in the woods," he'd said. "Instead of laptops we carry rifles.") Once he brought home some kind of bird that tasted suspiciously like chicken. He told Claudia it was pheasant, though quite young which might account for its mild taste.

Claudia didn't know what to think anymore. She didn't want a confrontation; she just wanted him to tell her the truth; no more of these stupid clues and hints. She suspected this was his way of telling her because he was too cowardly to just say it, to just say he had met someone else and that he wanted out. But she couldn't understand why he'd wait so long if he didn't love her anymore, if he didn't want to be with her. And why was *she* waiting so long? She was getting tired of being suspicious, of looking at every little thing he did as though it were filled with hidden meaning or a confession of guilt. Guilty until proven innocent. She had always been a suspicious type; she got it from her mother.

— • —

A couple of summers ago Claudia was on a beach reading a paperback and occasionally looking up at the small waves lapping against the wet sand. The sky was cloudless and brilliant; the sunlight shimmered and danced across the water. And the sand between her toes was warm and dry. It was her idea of pure happiness: alone on a beach with a book, not a soul in sight. Barry was off somewhere probably sleeping in the shade. He hated the sun.

Claudia looked up from her book at one point and noticed a man approaching her. He had come from nowhere. He was pale and thin, and wore a white shirt, open at the chest, a large brimmed hat and sunglasses. He was holding a geologist's hammer and a magnifying glass in his hands. She looked back into her book and waited for him to pass. But he stopped in front of her and cleared his throat.

"Pardon me," the man said.

Claudia looked up with an expression of mixed suspicion and curiousity. Now that he was closer, she saw that he was sweating profusely. The short, curly hair on his chest was wet with perspiration. And the damp curly hair on his head stuck out from the sides of his hat in a clownish sort of way.

"Yes?"

"Is your name Claudia? Claudia Gaines?"

Upon first looking at the man, Claudia did not recognize him at all. She hadn't a clue who he might be. Or why he might know her name. She squinted her eyes up at him dubiously; she was suspicious of his intentions. What was he doing on the beach all by himself, anyway? No, she decided, something didn't seem right.

"No. Sorry." She looked back down into her book. But the man persisted.

"I'm sorry. I could have sworn.... Weren't you just in the offices of Lamb and Hartley applying for a temp job last week? You would have met with Ms. Cornell, I believe."

Claudia looked back up at the man slowly. She closed her book without marking the page. Now she recognized him. Button up the shirt, put on a jacket and tie, take off the hat, the sunglasses. Replace the hammer with a pen, the magnifying glass with a stack of files....

"Oh...Oh. Yes." She felt her face redden. She looked past him at the water and imagined herself out there on a life raft, floating out to sea. Helpless, but thankfully alone.

"So...you *are* Claudia then? Norm Hill. Remember? We met by the elevator." He held out his hand and smiled. "I'm usually pretty good with remembering faces."

There wasn't much else to say at that point. Norm seemed to be waiting for an explanation for why Claudia denied who she was. But Claudia couldn't think of one. She smiled. And then Norm walked off.

She got the job, and, with her head down, she walked into the offices of Lamb and Hartley Monday morning. Norm didn't say anything about their meeting on the beach. He smiled and walked past her in the hall.

— • —

Maybe she was being paranoid like that day on the beach. Maybe it was all a mistake.

On the day of her birthday, Claudia stopped at the supermarket to pick up a cake on her way home from work. Barry usually got one, but this year he said he was too busy with work to get to the supermarket on time. He said he felt bad asking but they just had to have a cake. Claudia didn't really want one, but her mother was coming over and Barry insisted on having a little something to mark her birthday.

"This is a big one, hun. You gotta go into the forties with a bang," he said.

In the check-out line Claudia picked up a women's magazine that caught her eye. One of the articles was titled, "How to tell if your man is cheating." The cover showed a buxom blonde in a revealing gown that would have made it difficult for her to walk. She had a pouty, far away look on her face, as if someone had just told her that her boyfriend was cheating on her and she was trying to decide what to wear to their final date. Half way down the page, Claudia read, "How to keep your man coming back for more." She threw the magazine down alongside the cake.

Outside, Claudia put her bag on a bench and sat down. One of the first tell-tale signs that your man is cheating, she read, is frequent bathing: "To rid himself of the smell of another woman's sex." Put that way, it made Claudia want to vomit. She had noticed Barry bathing more than usual. He was always showering. Staying late after work and then coming in smelling like alcohol ("Went out with the guys for a beer.") or smelling like whatever else. And then showering. He went through a bar of soap a week. She had been so naïve.

It sounded cheap. It sounded accurate. She finished the article and dropped the magazine into a garbage can on her way home.

— • —

Claudia's mother, Bea, was waiting on the front steps when Claudia got home from the supermarket.

"You were supposed to be here half an hour ago," she said. And then added, "Happy birthday."

Bea was as short as Claudia was tall. She had curly gray hair and red, always rosy red cheeks. She looked like someone's grandmother, which, to her chagrin, she wasn't.

Bea got up off the stairs and picked up her parcels.

"When my birthday comes, Claudia, I'm going to ask for just one thing. Do you know what that might be?"

"Yes, mom. I have a pretty good idea." Claudia was searching for her keys.

"Well, my birthday is in exactly nine months. What a coincidence. I worked out the math while I was waiting for you to get home. Nine months. Do you know what else takes nine months to arrive?"

"Christ, mom. You talk to me like I'm five. I'm not one of your kindergarteners."

Bea taught at Forest Park Elementary School. She had been teaching for most of her life. She moved up and down every year. Kindergarten. One. Two. Like an aerobics workout. She planned to retire at the end of the year and take some time for herself. Claudia's father died shortly after Claudia turned thirty. Cancer. Bea took it hard, and Claudia suggested she retire then and live off his insurance and her own retirement savings. But teaching provided the distraction she needed, and after the necessary grieving, Bea got used to her new life. The only thing she longed for now was a grandchild. Though despite this desire to be a grandmother, Bea remained somewhat cold towards Barry. She had a difficult time being supportive of Claudia marrying a man who had already been married once before. ("Once that we know of, anyway.")

And that was why Claudia didn't tell her mother about her suspicions. She was embarrassed, and so she found herself always making excuses for Barry, defending him. Nights when Bea called late and asked where Barry was, Claudia would get defensive and tell her mother how busy he was at work, what with that project they were preparing for the Pentagon and everything—the project that seemed to go on and on. Barry worked for a computer software firm. He knew nothing about computers when he first got the job, but it didn't matter because he was in sales. It didn't matter either that he was slow to learn; he knew how to sell a product, any product, and he could fake it. In more ways than one.

It was in that same office that Claudia met Barry five years ago. Before that, she was seeing a guy on and off for years—the surprise birthday party-er. They had discussed starting a family but Claudia couldn't imagine having children in such an unstable relationship. One minute they were on and everything was clear and bright; the next minute, clouds moved in and settled for a long, hard rain. He was an actor/waiter. A waiting actor, Claudia called him. Then there was Barry.

She was temp-ing back then. When the secretary in Barry's office left on maternity leave, Claudia filled in for her, picking things up as she went along. While she was there, Barry hung around her desk and flirted, asking her out and leaving notes on her in-tray. Claudia knew he was married, but he told her that he and his wife were living separately, waiting for the divorce to come through— all of which was more or less accurate. Before long Claudia was smitten. She found his flirting—despite the wife and kids he had at home—very flattering, even romantic. She had never received that kind of attention before. There had been at least half a dozen other boyfriends. All nice enough guys in their own way, but lacking the intensity and passion Barry seemed to exhibit those first months. Barry was all fired up, full of excitement and spontaneity; he was a good-time guy. Some of their first dates involved driving down the coast to some secluded B & B, where they'd spend a romantic evening drinking and talking, skinny dipping and then making love on the beach. Once even on a picnic table. She felt like a teenager whenever they were together.

And then he started drifting a little, like a boat not anchored. He said it was because of work, the pressure to move forward, to keep up. Claudia moved from job to job while Barry got more and more involved in his work. It was not unusual now for them to go days without talking or seeing one another except mornings before leaving for work—Barry had taken to sleeping on the couch when he got home late. ("Didn't want to wake you," he'd say in the morn- ing.) But then he would surprise her, come home with flowers and plans and all full of love and compliments—he was often drunk those nights.

— • —

Bea scolded her daughter for buying her own birthday cake.

"I would have made one, had I known you'd be buying your own."

"Buy it. Bake it. What's the difference?"

"Where is that man? Shouldn't he be here by now?"

"He'll be here soon. He just had to finish up at work."

"Honestly, Claudia. I wonder about him sometimes."

"Not now, please."

Bea was unwrapping her famous potato salad. She still kept secret some of the ingredients—which was why she insisted on making it at home and not at Claudia's. She also brought deviled eggs, a chicken pie (Barry's favourite) and a box of chicken wings (Claudia's favourite). Claudia threw together a green salad, violently chopping carrots and imagining that they were other things, like fingers or toes. She reached over and turned on the radio to drown out the constant drone of her mother's voice. Talking, always talking. About school, about the kids, about grandchildren. About Claudia's errant husband.

"Where is he anyway?" Bea said, leaning over the counter to look out the window. "Not once did your father forget my birthday."

"He didn't forget. He just didn't have time to get the cake."

Claudia wondered why she continued to defend him like this. It was humiliating.

"You seem a little out of it today. I hope you don't mind me saying. What are you dreaming about? That trip to Florida we're going to take one of these days?"

"No, mom. I'm not dreaming of Florida."

"I'll get you there some day."

The truth was Claudia thought Florida was tacky, the most pathetic state of them all. But she never said so to Bea. It was Florida,

Claudia knew, that helped her mother through her grieving. Still, she had no plans to ever go there. And she had to come up with an excuse every year.

"Your father would have loved Florida. Now there was an honest and caring and loving husband." Bea stopped what she was doing and gazed out the window.

"I know, mom."

"Well, you know what they say?" Bea turned back to her potato salad and gave it a quick stir. "God loves a broken heart."

"Who are *they*?" Claudia nicked her finger but there was no blood.

"The Buddhists."

"The Buddhists say that? Are you sure?"

"Yes, the Buddhists."

Bea put the potato salad on the table and began unwrapping the eggs. She hummed while she worked, and it sounded to Claudia like the wings of a hummingbird. Or a hundred monks in a distant valley simultaneously saying "Om."

Claudia finished the salad, covered it with clear wrap and put it in the fridge. She excused herself from her mother who was still talking and went to her room to change. She closed the door behind her and sat on the bed. There was no one she could talk to. She wished she had a sister or a best friend. But she had neither. Her only best friend got married and moved away to Toronto. They spoke on the phone now and then, whenever Claudia called her. But distance did something to their friendship, marriage and distance. Claudia thought about Toronto. It was the kind of city she could imagine moving to and getting lost in with all the other lost souls. She'd get a little apartment, change her name, her hair colour and then…. But why bother? Who'd come looking for her anyway? She got up and slipped off her clothes and left them in a pile on the floor. She looked at herself in the mirror.

"I'm old," she said to her reflection.

She turned around and looked over her shoulder. She had managed to keep herself in good shape despite never getting any exercise. She tightened the muscles on her bum and poked at her cheeks. She walked over to the closet and got out some jeans and a white blouse. Bea could still be heard talking in the kitchen. On and on and on. Claudia was glad to not have any children now. Once upon a time she wanted many kids—five or six—but that was long ago. Lots of kids, a garden, a husband. That was all she ever wanted. That and a few other things. But those things in particular. Two out of three. One out of three: the garden wasn't doing too well this year. She just didn't have the time for it. Or the state of mind. She transferred her quiet rage into the roots of all the plants. They were slowly dying of negative energy; shriveling up and keeling over. She applied some lipstick and brushed her hair.

"Forty," she whispered. "Every inch of me is forty years old."

She planned to ask him point-blank, over dinner and with her mother as a witness, is there another woman? It seemed so easy. In theory. Then one way or another, she could get on with her life. End of story. Or beginning. But there was a feeling tugging away at her insides like a small child tugging at her mother's skirt. *What will I do if he lies?* she wondered. *If he tells the truth?*

The rumble of Barry's truck became audible. He was coming around the corner and approaching their driveway. Claudia watched through the mirror, which reflected the open window in her room. The truck turned into the driveway, the motor cut out and the door opened and closed. And then it was quiet but for the hum of her mother's voice.

Bea was setting the table when Claudia entered the kitchen. Barry came in calling out for the birthday girl. He was in one of those moods. He walked over to Claudia with a bouquet of flowers and gave her a hug that she accepted with her arms hanging limp at her sides. She sniffed at the air around him for the smell of alcohol or perfume.

"Lordy, lordy, look who's forty," he said.

"Hi."

"You're chipper," Bea said.

"Of course I am. It's my wife's birthday. Did you get the cake?"

Claudia nodded. Bea glared at him but he didn't appear to notice.

"Sorry I couldn't get to it. I had a shit load of work to get through. But I got it done and the rest of the night is yours. We'll do whatever you want to do. Anything at all."

Barry sat down to untie his shoes. He kicked them off towards the door. He wasn't a big man, not much bigger than Bea except for the gut divided from his lower body by a belt that was always cinched one notch too tight. He had sandy blond hair and a slightly blotchy complexion. Claudia tried to imagine another woman being interested in sleeping with this man. But she knew with a man like him it wasn't only his appearance. In fact, it wasn't his appearance at all. It was his charm. His charisma. That's what got her. He set his sights on her, and didn't give up until...until now.

He loosened his tie and hung his coat over the back of the chair.

Claudia leaned against the fridge door and wondered who it was. Some temp slut? Is that what she had been? Some new hire: young, talented, fresh out of school and looking for *experience*? She knew it wasn't anyone his own age or even her age for that matter. Some tramp who knows he's married and doesn't care. Claudia thought about following him after work some evening. Dressing in black, the way kids do these days, from head to toe. And then she'd wait for him to leave the office; she'd track him like a dog, like a hunter—a mercenary. But how could she ever do any of that? He was the one who watched the James Bond movies, not her; he was the one who read the Tom Clancy novels. It wasn't her style. She felt deflated.

"Claudia? Claudia?" Bea was calling her.

"What?"

"Will you get the salad out of the fridge? Barry and I are starving."

·She got the salad and some pop. The rest of the table was set and waiting.

Barry looked at her with a crooked smile.

"This is just great. I'm so happy," he said.

"That makes only two of us," Bea said. "Claudia, you haven't said one word yet. It's only forty, Claudia. Believe me, that's not old."

"Claudia, hun, forty is child's play. You want old, you should have seen this guy who came into the office today—"

"Is there a new temp in the office?" Claudia stared at him accusingly as she spoke.

"No." Barry looked at her quizzically as he bit into a chicken wing.

Bea asked him how his work was going. Claudia didn't listen to his answer. She knew it by heart already: *Great. This new project we have coming down the pipe is really going to be big. The real thing....*

She looked over at him. He was stuffing food into his mouth while he spoke. She poked at her potato salad with her fork. She hadn't even touched the chicken wings. Nothing seemed to make sense on her plate. Green salad, chicken wings, potato salad, the eggs, the pie.... It made no sense aesthetically or gastronomically. And she realized it was always like this. They sat down to some hodgepodge meal, talked about Florida or Barry's day at work or whatever and then cleared the table, ate the cake and sat in front of the TV with a cup of coffee. It was the same thing every year. Every goddamn year.

Claudia pushed her chair away from the table.

"I need some air. I'll be right back."

Bea and Barry looked at her. And then at one another. Barry nodded as if he knew what was up. Claudia knew that meant he thought she had her period or it was because of turning forty. He looked back down at his plate and stabbed at a piece of chicken pie with his fork.

"Fuck you," she said quietly. It didn't come out sounding angry, but final, in the way one might say *So long* or *Good-bye*.

Barry furrowed his brow. Bea sat there and looked at Claudia. She looked old sitting there, with a half-eaten deviled egg between her fingers, and a thin string of spittle between the egg and her mouth. Claudia looked at her mother sadly. She noticed her getting older right before her eyes. They were all getting older. And for what? What was there to look forward to? Florida every winter for two fun-filled weeks? Another temp job? Nothing was making sense. On her way out the door, she picked up Barry's keys from the key hook.

The neighbour across the street was out drowning his lawn again. He sat on his porch with the hose in his hand, rotating it like an oscillating fan. He waved at Claudia when he heard the door close behind her. She tried to smile. She walked down the three steps to the front lawn. It was a small yard, surrounded by a thin, short hedge. The flowers she had planted beside the porch were just a few inches tall and a step closer to death every day.

Why are you doing this to me? What is wrong with me? She wanted to speak her mind, say what she was thinking. But why start now? She thought of running. As a child, she ran off and hid anytime her father raised his voice to her. Under beds, behind chairs, in trees. She once hid under her father's car, secretly hoping he would start it and run her over. And then he'd feel bad he ever yelled at her. And over what? What had it been? Running into the street without looking? Not eating everything on her plate? Talking back? It didn't matter now. Just like *this* wouldn't matter in thirty years.

Barry's truck was blocking her car in the driveway. There was no way she could drive off into the sunset. Drive to Toronto and find her best friend Carol, tell her everything. The more she thought about it, the more ridiculous it sounded—moving to Toronto. What kind of city was it anyway? It was a mess of bad air and tall buildings. Even Florida seemed better. She'd have to choose some other city, in some other country. Or another neighbourhood, at least.

She walked around the edge of the yard to the driveway and stood looking at the truck. It was getting old. There were dents in the fender, rust around the wheel wells. The bumper looked like all it needed was one good kick to bring it to its knees. So she kicked it. But it stayed hanging on. Some rust fell from underneath and landed at her feet. Rotting. *Everything is rotting from the inside out around here.* The back of the truck was filled with papers and trash and fast food containers. Standing there peering into the back of the truck, snooping around like that, Claudia felt stupid and unloved.

She walked around to the driver's side and opened up the door. A stale odour escaped; it smelled like greasy food and cigarette smoke. She climbed in and closed the door. In the rear-view mirror, she could see the man watering his lawn across the street; he was watching her now. She leaned over and opened the glove compartment. It was crammed with maps and pens and receipts and loose papers. Claudia emptied it onto the floor. Hid away at the back, tucked under an empty pack of cigarettes, was a small opened box of condoms.

"Fuckfuckfuckbastardfucker."

She wanted to light the truck on fire or send it careening off a cliff. She wanted to run her husband over with it. She put the key in the ignition and started the truck. It was a stick shift. Her little Civic was an automatic. It roared and stunk like diesel. She put the truck into reverse and looked out the back window. The man across the street was watching her, holding the hose at his side so that it was spraying not the lawn but his driveway. The truck rolled out onto the street and then stalled. Bea was standing at the door waving to Claudia. Not waving "hello" but waving "what-the-hell-are-you-doing?" Claudia ignored her, got the truck started again and then put it into first gear. She thought of leaving, but how far could she get in a truck she didn't know how to drive? And where would she go anyway?

But then for a second everything made sense. For a split second it was clear. She knew she was doing the right thing. She saw things in the way people who are close to death see their past. Only she saw her future, every second of it, and it was long and joyous. It was sunshine and beaches, cheap romance novels and sun-hats. It was supper waiting on the table for her when she got home from work.

The future was a real man.

She revved the engine. Barry was at the door yelling. She read his lips, "What the hell...." She thought about how he and her mother had a lot in common. Maybe that's why at that moment, looking at them standing there together, she hated them both. She turned the wheels to face the house, the front door, and then she let the clutch pop back up. The truck lurched forward. She pushed the accelerator all the way down and held on tight. She crashed through the hedges, and onto the front lawn. The truck jerked forward over the grass, crushing the flowers and then smashing into the porch. And then it stalled. The engine died down. Everyone was silent.

The future...the real man....

Claudia's forehead was stinging and hot. She brought her fingers to her head and when she looked at them, they were red with blood. She looked out the window and up into the sky. She thought she saw a balloon, perhaps released from some child's hand, rise up into the blue sky. She leaned forward in her seat and looked up. But she couldn't see anything. Some clouds, a darkening sky. No balloon. And then she thought she saw it again, rising up and up. She thought she saw a lot of things floating up into the sky. There were voices, too: a man's and a woman's, but they were far away. A red balloon.... She reached out for it but her hand hit the windshield, and then it was gone. And all that remained was a terrible noise pulsing in her head. She stayed there for a long time, just trying to remember what the future looked like.

MEAT

M itchell turned from the woman getting dressed in the corner of the room and looked outside. The light from the red motel sign was refracted through the small droplets of rain on the dirty window. The raindrops gathered like insects, shimmering for an instant before sliding down the face of the window in an endless procession. The rain had been falling steadily for two days. When Mitchell entered the motel room the night before, he told the woman he wasn't leaving until the rain stopped. "Even if it takes forty days and forty nights," he'd said. He was drunk at the time and stumbled across the room to the bed. The woman giggled and closed the door behind her; she was not nearly as drunk as he. Mitchell opened the drawer of the bedside table and pulled out a bible. The spine cracked when he opened its pages. He read aloud: "And God blessed Noah and his sons, and said unto them, Be fruitful, and multiply, and replenish the earth.... Every moving thing that liveth shall be meat for you." He slammed the book shut and threw it in the drawer, laughing. The woman laughed, too, and then began to undress.

It was now close to dawn and the light on the horizon was murky and distant. The rain continued to fall; the wind blew in from the west. There was a sound at the window like small pebbles being thrown at the glass from somewhere below. The room was on the second floor facing the parking lot and the street beyond, and beyond that the used car dealerships and gas stations and strip malls that lined the street. There was a haze over all of this, like smoke over a crowded barroom table. The clouds above, blending seamlessly with the haze, were dark and oppressive. Mitchell considered getting up and leaving, but lay there instead, his mind wandering lazily to the night before and then further back, to a night when he was a small boy, of seven or eight.

His father had brought him to a bar not unlike the one where Mitchell met the woman who was now in his room. The bar was dark and cheap, the kind one sees but rarely stops at along unlit stretches of urban streets. Mitchell's father was not a drinking man, and until a few years before that night, he accompanied his family to church regularly. There were four children, and Mitchell was the youngest. His father was tall and sturdy and had spent most of his adult life working in the local saw mill. He seldom had time for his children, let alone his wife. That night he sat Mitchell on a stool and ordered two root beers. He had heard about a man who sold meat from a table in a back corner. The rumour was that the man worked for a packing company, and at the end of his shift, he secretly stuffed assorted meats into his shirt and pants. Afterwards, he would make his way to the bar and proceed to unburden himself of these meats piece by piece, selling them at a reduced rate. Mitchell's father had hoped that by having a child with him he would get an even cheaper price. The family was not poor, but Mitchell's father was a man who liked a deal.

There was, indeed, a man at the bar that night who sold meat from his shirt and pants. And Mitchell's father got the best price in the place. Mitchell's mother soon stopped buying meat at the supermarket, and the man and Mitchell's father became great friends. Mitchell only went to the bar that one time. After that, his father went alone. But that one night remained in his memory like a small polished gem: in the end, not worth very much, but valuable to the holder all the same. It was one of the few happy memories—or not unhappy, at any rate—that Mitchell had of his father. He could remember the feeling of being perched upon the stool, his feet dangling nearly two feet from the tiled floor. And the taste of the root beer, unlike any root beer he had ever tasted before. And then afterwards, the not unpleasant coarseness of his throat, his head swimming from the cigarette smoke that filled the room like fog.

After Mitchell's father finished his root beer, the meat-selling man bought him a regular beer. The two men drank straight from their bottles, and before long Mitchell's father was buying the next round. They laughed at one another's stories and shared tales of hardship and past exploits. They spoke loudly, unashamedly of women they had known. They made no effort to include Mitchell in their conversation but neither did they exclude him. He was present and they allowed him to listen, to laugh along, to be a part of the moment. He had never heard his father laugh so much, nor tell such stories. He had never seen his father drink beer before that night.

A few months after that, his father quit his job and went into business with the meat-selling man. They invested in a truck together and made a sign that read "Hank and Frank's Antiques and light moving", though neither man was named Hank nor Frank. They attended auctions outside of town and purchased antiques and collectibles. They turned a profit by selling what they bought to the over-priced shops in town. Mitchell's father would eventually leave his family and marry the meat-selling man's sister in Quebec.

Mitchell now saw his own life heading in the same direction as his father's: the less time he spent with his family, the less time he wanted to spend with them. After a while, he blamed them for his unhappiness, and it became an excuse for his infidelities. Instead of trying to turn the boat around, Mitchell picked up an oar and paddled hopelessly away from shore. He thought of this as he looked back at the woman in the corner of the room. She was singing quietly now, some popular song. Her feet tapped out the rhythm in an uneven tempo as she brushed her hair, pinned it back. Her purse lay on the chair next to the window, her shoes were near the door, beside Mitchell's. She asked him what he was thinking about. Her face was mottled by the light coming in through the window. She was pretty but older than she had at first appeared the night before. Mitchell smiled at her, and shook his head. "Nothing," he said. "Nothing at all." Before long, he dressed and said good-bye.

THE SAD DARK EYES OF A DEAD DOG

In 1977 my family rented a small house at the top of a small hill in the suburbs. It would be one of the last times we'd all live together under the same roof, but of course we didn't know that then. The house I'm thinking of was surrounded by other houses that looked—if one were new to the neighborhood—exactly the same. My father often joked that after a long day at work he would walk into the wrong house, crawl into the wrong bed and cuddle up to the wrong wife. He loved this joke, and it made my mother blush every time he said it. They got along well that summer. This was before he finally decided he wanted to be on his own.

We had a driveway and a porch and a yard with the small tin shed my father used as a study. These were things we never had before, things my parents were proud to possess—however tenuously. I sat on the porch nearly every day of that summer: reading and playing with bugs and watching the neighbors come and go. They said hello as they strolled by the house. The old woman across the street, Mrs. Taylor, waved to me with her short, fleshy arm as she reached for her mail in the morning. It was one of the few times I saw her venture outdoors and even then it was really only her arm that left the house.

And there were our next door neighbours, the Hendersons. Every time Mr. Henderson cut the lawn that summer—he did so at least once a week—he would also cut his son's hair with electric clippers in front of their house. Matthew sat perfectly still, obeying his father's commands: *"Forward!" "To the left!" "To the right!"* I would sit on our porch and watch the hair fall from Matthew's head down to the fresh-cut lawn. Grass and hair clippings blew away with the slightest breeze, barely noticed unless, turned at a particular angle, the grass caught the light of the sun and glinted back at you. Even then, who really noticed those things?

— • —

The day before leaving for the family cottage that summer, Matthew asked me if I wanted to go along. The idea of spending time at the Henderson's cottage was only somewhat appealing to me. Matthew could be a confounding bully, knocking me down one minute and calling me his pal the next. And his parents.... His parents were another thing all together. But I had never been to a cottage. And then there was the lake. And not just any lake but a big lake, teeming with crayfish and snails, sunfish and frogs. I had only ever seen most of these things in books.

At night, Matthew told me, you could lie on the small dock his father had built two summers before and listen to fish jumping out of the lake to catch insects at the surface. They flew through the cool night air and landed back in the water with a quiet splash. You listened to this, he explained, while lying on your back looking up at the night sky, watching the millions of stars you can see in the country sky. And if you were not careful walking back to the cottage after all of this, if the stars were still in your eyes, you might trip on a raccoon or a porcupine. Sometimes, in the mornings, they were still out there wandering around, dazed by the morning light.

If you're really lucky, Matthew told me, lowering his voice and looking around secretively, you might see a fox or a deer. But only if you're really lucky.

Matthew had never spoken so poetically about anything. It must be, I remember thinking, the real thing. It sounded like paradise, like something you read about in a book: lazy and hot, fishing off the dock. And a dock that Matthew's father had built with his own hands. The only thing my dad ever made was a small clay ashtray. He was jokingly proud of it and showed it to anyone who came to visit. But a dock...that was something to be proud of. Matthew's father began to seem like a decent guy.

Despite the company—and trying not to act too excited—I told Matthew I'd like very much to go. I left him on our front porch and ran in to ask my parents for permission. Both my mom and dad said it sounded like a great idea. They were happy I would be able to get out to the country, even if it was with the Hendersons. It was something they would have liked to have done themselves. I called to Matthew through the screen door and told him the good news.

"See you in the morning," he said, and then jumped over the railing of our porch—something which annoyed my mother to no end—and ran across the lawn back home.

— • —

Morning came and I sat out on the front porch with my dad's old sleeping bag, a pillow and an over-stuffed duffel bag. I had never packed for this type of trip before, so I brought just about everything I could fit into the bag. Before long the Hendersons began packing their station wagon. Matthew came out of the house with a fishing rod and a net in his hands and a backpack hanging from one shoulder. He quickly glanced my way and then looked over at his mother who was watching him. I was trying to pick up my stuff. I nodded my head and smiled at them both. Matthew threw his fishing equipment and bag into the back of the car and ran across our lawn.

"Hey, David," he said, climbing over the railing of our porch. "I guess you can't come after all. There's not enough room. Sorry."

He looked at his mother while telling me this, and spoke loud enough so that she could hear. I glanced over at her and she turned away. Matthew leaned in close and quietly whispered in my ear.

"My mom's worried you might drown. You know, 'cuz you can't swim? And then your parents would sue my parents for all we've got. Well, see ya."

He said this with the matter-of-factness of a thirteen-year-old-toughie, and then he shrugged his shoulders and ran back to the car. It was true, I couldn't swim, had never learned how. There was nothing I could say.

If Mrs. Henderson had been watching us, she did so inconspicuously, taking advantage of her dark glasses. Mr. Henderson honked the horn and Matthew's sister, Melanie, waved from the back seat of the car as they passed by the front of our house.

I let my luggage fall and sat back down. I looked over at Mrs. Taylor's house. The curtains were all drawn; the lawn was overgrown and full of weeds. The house looked deserted. A car slowly drove past, and the driver looked over at me and nodded. Another car started up our one-way street the wrong way but turned around and sped off. The street was quiet.

— • —

After a while, I gathered the courage to go inside and face my family. I quietly opened the door and placed my things inside the hall. My mom was in her bathrobe, looking out the back window and drinking coffee from a mug with the words "Super Dad" printed in black lettering on the side.

"The birds are eating all the grass seed," she said without looking at me.

"Oh," I said.

She turned to face me.

"I was beginning to think you left without saying good-bye. Are you leaving now?"

"No. Not going," I muttered.

"Why not?"

"No room. They already left."

I looked down at my shoes. They were still stained green from the last time I mowed the lawn. I ran over the extension cord and my dad had to buy a new one. I looked back up at my mom. My face felt hot.

"They what?"

"They left. They said there was no room. It's okay."

"Okay? That's not okay. Those lousy-no-good-for-nothing.... How could they do that to you? I can't believe this."

A small blue vein started to swell on her forehead.

"It's okay, Mom. Really. I don't even care."

"No. Oh, no. They're gonna hear about this when they get back. What a...what a...bitch! I can't believe her."

She nearly spilled her coffee on the floor, she was so angry.

"Will! Will!" she called. "Where's your father?"

Dad came into the kitchen wearing his pajamas and carrying a newspaper.

"What's going on?" he asked.

My mom explained to him what had happened.

"They what?"

He slammed his newspaper down on the table as if he were acting in a high school play: it was dramatic, to be sure, but somewhat amateurish. He was not one to show much emotion.

My sister, Tina, who had been sitting silently at the table eating her breakfast and reading the side of the cereal box, looked up at Dad and made a clicking sound with her tongue.

"Jeez, David," he said. "I'm really sorry. God, how could they get your hopes up like that? I'll tell you what. We'll go to a…a lake on the weekend and rent a canoe. How 'bout it?"

"Yeah, sure."

I knew my dad well enough to know not to put any faith in his promises. But I tried to smile all the same.

"They're a buncha shits anyway," said Tina.

"Tina!"

My mom slammed her hand down on the table.

"Well, you called Mrs. Henderson a bitch."

"That doesn't excuse you from using that kind of language."

"That's hardly fair.…"

I slipped out the back door and into the yard.

There were some birds eating the grass seed my dad had thrown down absently. I tried to scare them away but they only flew up onto the wires over my head and waited for me to leave. The lawn was sparse, with bald patches here and there, and a worn-down trail leading from the house to my father's study. I stood scarecrow-still for a moment and waited to see if the birds would come back down for the seed. But they remained perched on the wires, watching me with their little black eyes until I went back inside.

— • —

During supper, I asked if I could camp out in the shed that night.

"Study," my dad corrected me.

They still felt pretty bad about what the Hendersons had done so they said sure. Tina snickered. After sunset, I gathered my things from where I had let them fall that morning and went out to the back yard. The sky was turning dark but only two stars were visible. It was pitch black inside the shed. For authenticity's sake, I didn't want to turn my dad's lamp on, so I got out my flashlight and used its light to get ready for bed. I laid out my sleeping bag and pillow and pulled out an old issue of *National Geographic* from my duffel bag. Once everything was arranged, I read about the darkling bee-tle by the light of my flashlight. The darkling beetle remains still all night, waiting for dew to form on its back. At day break, as conden-sation builds upon its shiny exoskeleton, the beetle tilts its body forward, sending water down its body, into its mouth. I closed the magazine and turned off the flashlight. I envisioned a thousand darkling beetles lined up outside, waiting for dawn. And I thought about the lake at Matthew's cottage, about the raccoons and the stars. When I closed my eyes, I could see the Henderson's car driv-ing away without me, and Matthew sitting in the back seat, pre-tending not to see me on the porch surrounded by my camping gear. I vowed to learn how to swim, to show them they had made a mistake by leaving me behind. Somewhere on the other side of the thin aluminum wall near my head, a cricket chirped.

— • —

The Hendersons returned home three weeks later. The bot-tom half of their car was covered with dust and mud. The grill was thick with dead bugs. I sat on the sidewalk with a magnifying glass watching ants. They scrambled around looking for their home while hopelessly trying to dig new holes in the warm, hard concrete. I put the magnifying glass down in their path to divert them but they simply walked over or around it. The Hendersons began unpacking their car. Melanie ran over to where I sat.

"Hi," she said.

"Hi."

"Whatcha doin'?"

"Melanie, get over here and help us unpack," Mrs. Henderson called.

Melanie ran back to the car and wrapped her arms around a large purple and yellow sleeping bag and carried it into the house. Matthew looked over at me and tentatively raised his hand to wave. I looked back down at the ants. One had found the remains of a dead sow bug and was walking in circles with the thing on its back. I knocked the carcass off the ant and flicked it away with my finger. I glanced over at the Hendersons. They were all busy carrying things in. Just looking at them, I could smell campfires and fresh-air. I knelt down close to the ants and blew them all off the sidewalk, like blowing out candles on a birthday cake. The Hendersons continued unpacking their car.

At the corner of our street a big blue car screeched to a halt. The fender on the driver's side was rusty and dented; all the windows were tinted and rolled up. It idled there for a moment with the engine rumbling. I looked quickly to see if the Hendersons were watching. They were. The driver's side door opened, and the driver threw a green garbage bag out onto the road. It happened so quickly, and so unexpectedly, that I could only see that the driver was a man, and that he wore a hat which shaded his eyes. After that, the door slammed shut and the car sped off down the hill.

Matthew and I were the first to reach the bag. It was torn open and in the bag was a dog, black and bloody and, of course, dead. I stepped back from it quickly. I thought I was going to throw up. The rest of Matthew's family ran over to see what it was.

"Oh, dear," Mrs. Henderson said, turning away.

Melanie peered at the dog from behind her mother's legs. Mr. Henderson looked down at the dog and then at Matthew and me.

Matthew looked up.

"We'll bury it," he said, looking back at the dog.

I looked at him and then down at the dog. My throat was dry and my jaw tingled the way it always did before I threw up.

"Where?" I managed to ask, somehow pushing back the feeling of having to vomit.

"In our yard."

"No you're not," said his mother. "Not in our yard you're not."

"We can do it in my yard," I said, and then thought about what my mom would say. But it was too late.

Matthew picked up the bag and started walking towards my house. I followed close behind. My mom wasn't going to like this. I took the lead and we went around back. Matthew let the bag fall in the middle of the yard.

"Gotta shovel?"

"Just one," I said.

"I'll go get one from our place."

He jumped the fence and ran over to their shed.

"Don't jump over the fence," his mother called from the driveway. "And you come help us unload the car before you bury that thing."

Matthew looked back at me and laughed.

All the grass seed in our yard was gone. So were the birds. I decided I had better tell my mom what we planned to do. I found her in the kitchen peeling potatoes and listening to the radio. She was swaying to the music and humming along. I cleared my throat and waited for her to stop. Without looking up and without missing a beat to the music she spoke.

"What are you—oh, shit. Grab a cloth from the sink. I went and spilled starchy water on my slacks."

I rinsed out the cloth sitting in the sink and handed it to her.

She cleaned off her pants and smiled at me.

"What's up? Are the Henderson's back?"

"Yes."

"I thought I heard their car."

"Oh, no. That wasn't their car. Some guy just drove by and threw a garbage bag with a dead dog in it out his door and Matthew and I are going to bury it in the back yard. Is that okay?"

"What?"

"A dog...a dead dog. We're going to bury it in the back yard. If that's okay...."

I looked up at her with big sad eyes.

"You're going to bury it here?" She pointed toward the yard with the potato peeler.

"Yeah. Is that okay?"

"Jesus, David. In our yard?"

"Yeah. There's nowhere else."

"What about the Henderson's yard?"

"Uh, no room."

She looked out the window to the yard and back down at me. She took a deep breath.

"David.... Does it have to be here?"

"We have to, Mom. There's nowhere else."

"Oh, David. All right. But I don't want to see it. And not near my garden."

She took another deep breath and shook her head slowly from side to side.

"Where's your sister?"

"I don't know."

She pulled the curtain closed and went back to peeling potatoes.

— • —

I went out to the shed to get a shovel. The sliding aluminum
doors were open a crack and I could smell cigarette smoke coming
from inside.

"Dad?"

I wedged my hand between the doors and opened them enough
to see inside. Tina was sitting on my dad's small desk with her feet
on his chair and a cigarette in her hand. She quickly hid the cigarette behind her back and jumped off the desk. When she saw that
I was alone, she brought the cigarette back to her mouth and inhaled deeply. She closed her mouth and motioned me over with her
free hand. I didn't move right away.

"Are you going to hit me?" I asked.

She shook her head no. I knew her better than that, but I
took a few steps forward all the same. When I got close enough, she
reached around to the back of my head with her free hand and pulled
my face into hers. With her lips on mine she blew smoke into my
mouth and laughed. I fell back on my ass, coughing and spitting.

Tina smiled down at me and slowly inhaled again from her
cigarette.

"You'd better not say a word to Mom and Dad," she said, smoke
lazily drifting from her open mouth, "cuz they'll smell it on your
breath, too."

She butted out her cigarette and stepped over me.

"If anybody asks, I'll be at Wendy's."

She slid the doors open all the way and walked out into the
sunlight. I spat on the ground one more time and looked around the

shed. The shovel was leaning against the wall in the corner; it prob-
ably hadn't been used in months. I grabbed it and stepped outside.
Tina stood near the garbage bag, moving it around with her foot.
The dog was covered up so that she couldn't see it.

"What's this?"

"A dead dog."

"Gross." She stepped away from it. "Where the hell did it
come from?"

"Some guy threw it out of his car. It was already dead. Matthew and I are gonna bury it."

"Good for you. See ya later."

She turned and walked away.

— • —

I started digging a hole in the far corner of the yard, away
from my mom's garden. Matthew came back and started poking at
the hole with his shovel. I could tell by the stupid grin on his face
that he had seen Tina. He had a crush on her.

"Tina has nice tits, eh?" Matthew grinned and looked up at
me.

"Shut up."

We dug about three and half feet down before stopping. Matthew put his shovel down and wiped his forehead.

"Well...."

We looked at one another and then down at the bag. Matthew poked at it with the toe of his shoe until we could see the dog.
Its fur was damp and matted and crusty. And its eyes were stuck
wide open, dark and sad. It looked like a car had hit it. I felt sick for
it, the poor thing.

Matthew reached down and touched it. His finger turned red
and glistened in the sunlight.

"Look," he said.

"I see. Come on. Let's just bury it. That's disgusting."

"You think it's disgusting?" he asked.

He reached down again and ran his hand over the dog's damp fur. He brought his hand up to my face and smeared the blood on my cheek.

"You asshole."

"What'd you call me?"

Without waiting for an answer, he reached down a third time, covered his hand in blood and smeared it across my mouth. It tasted dirty and stung my lips. In a rage, I raised the shovel to knock Matthew's hand away from my face. But I swung it too high and hit him right in the head. He spun around and lost his footing, falling to the ground next to the dog. Blood started oozing from the cut on his head.

"Oh, no," was all I could say.

I began to feel faint and leaned heavily on my shovel. Matthew was crying and cursing and holding the cut above his brow. I just stood there, watching him, unable to move. He looked up at me through the blood and tears, and turned quiet for a second. Then he got up and started running with his hands on his head, the blood pouring down.

"Mommmm," he screamed all the way out of the yard.

My mom came running out the back door. She must have been about to pour herself a glass of lemonade because she had the pitcher and a glass in her hands. When she saw Matthew run by with his face and hands covered in blood, she looked over at me. Her expression turned from confusion to horror when she saw that my face was also covered in blood.

"What the hell happened out here?" she yelled.

"I...I hit Matthew on the head."

"With what?"

"With...a shovel."

"What's that on your face? Did he hit you?"

"No. It's the dog's blood. But he—"

She poured the entire pitcher of lemonade over my head, ice cubes and all. I stood there, gritting my teeth at the coldness of it. She put the pitcher and glass down on the bottom step and ran after Matthew.

I slowly made my way back to where the dog was. I covered it with the bag and picked it up. It was heavy, and I worried that it would fall out and land at my feet. But it didn't. And I awkwardly placed it in the hole and began shoveling dirt over it. When I finished, I patted the dirt down with the back of the shovel and tried to make it look just as it had before. The birds were back on the wire watching me. The blood and lemonade and sweat on my face were all beginning to dry and crack in the sun. I stood with my eyes closed for a moment and then went inside to clean up.

The house was quiet. My dad and Tina were both out. I changed my clothes and left them on the bathroom floor. Then I went back outside to wait for my mom to return. There was no sense in hiding. She'd find me.

— • —

My mom came around the corner and grabbed me by the arm. We started walking around the house toward the front.

"We are going over to Matthew's and you are going to apologize to him and his family for what you did."

"But he started it—"

"There is no excuse for hitting someone on the head with a shovel. My God, David. You could have killed him."

I resisted a little, but saw there was no use.

The Hendersons were sitting in lawn chairs on their front lawn. Two half-full tumblers of brandy were set out on a small, white table. Melanie was sitting on the grass playing with a doll. Matthew's head didn't look so bad. The blood was all cleaned up and his mom was holding an ice-pack to it. Mr. Henderson shook his head from side to side, watching me as I walked up the driveway and into their yard.

My mom placed me in front of the Hendersons and gave me a push.

"Say it."

"I'm really sorry I hit you on the head with the shovel, Matthew."

His mother made a little clucking noise and started shaking her head from side to side like Mr. Henderson.

I looked at Mrs. Henderson and then at Mr. Henderson and repeated, with a slight variation:

"I'm really sorry I hit Matthew on the head with the shovel, Mr. and Mrs. Henderson."

Mr. Henderson kept nodding his head, looking at me, and then up at my mom.

"May the Lord forgive you," he said.

Mrs. Henderson looked sullenly at Matthew and then glared up at me.

"That's enough. You've done enough damage for one day," she said.

Matthew had a pained expression on his face. He shrugged under the weight of the ice pack and looked down at the grass.

"I'm sorry about all of this," my mom said.

She took me by the arm and directed me out of the yard. Melanie looked up at me and smiled as I walked past.

Tina was home when we got there. She had found my wet, dirty clothes in the bathroom and asked what was going on. I shrugged my shoulders and went into my room. I could hear her and Mom talking outside my door. Tina laughed, and Mom said it wasn't funny. Then it was quiet. It would be a long time before I would learn how to swim.

PEOPLE LEAVING

When the woman sitting at the end of the bar began to cry, Walt decided to move over a few seats and talk to her. He had been watching her out of the corner of his eye for the past half-hour; watching her look down into her drink and then up at the other people in the bar, and occasionally at him sitting a few seats away. She reminded Walt of the kind of girl he would have been attracted to in high school, the kind of girl no one else would talk to or dance with. And Walt responded to her—just as he did with those other young women more than fifteen years ago—as one might respond to a small, wounded animal: instinctively, without giving it too much thought. That's how it began anyway.

She looked young, this woman, without necessarily being young. She wore glasses with tortoise-shell frames. There was a pimple on her chin. Her lime green sweater was similar to a style worn by high school girls: tight sleeves that were slightly too short. Walt thought of that old joke he often said to friends who were dating younger women. "She's so fresh out of high school," Walt would say, "you can still smell the pompoms on her hands." And then he would laugh. Ha ha ha ha ha.

But on this night Walt did not feel like laughing, and he only smiled half a smile; he was quiet and thoughtful. He had things on his mind, things he would sooner forget. He picked up his drink and swiveled his stool to face the woman. She looked up with a thin smile and shyly wiped the tears from her eyes with the sleeve of her sweater. Walt couldn't help but find this endearing. He smiled as he got up from his stool and walked over to the woman.

"Hello," he said.

"Hello," the woman said.

"I'm sorry to bother you but I.... Well, are you all right?"

The woman blushed.

"Yes. I'm fine. Thanks for asking. It was just the song playing on the radio. I found it sad."

Walt nodded his head thoughtfully and sat down next to her. The song was an old Motown hit he remembered from when he was a kid. It was a brokenhearted tune about lost love. But not so sad that it should cause one to break down crying within the first few bars—and in a public place. The music sounded far off, as though it were coming from another room and not from the speakers above their heads.

"I don't usually do things like this," the woman said. "I'm usually very reserved. It's just tonight...." She looked down at her drink, still embarrassed, and then picked up her glass. "It just reminded me," she said between sips, "of something sad."

Walt didn't know what to say next, so he drank from his glass and smiled at her with what he thought was a sad smile. She did the same and then looked out the window.

"It's just...things don't always work out the way you think they will, you know?"

She turned and looked at Walt intensely. Walt looked away—out the window and then into his drink. His hands were dirty and grease-stained from working on his car. He tried to hide them by covering the left with the right. And then the right with the left.

"Yeah," he said. "Tell me about it."

He stared at his hands and thought about his wife. He wondered if she was trying to call him at home now.

"Do you have a song like that?" the woman asked.

"Pardon?"

"A song like that. One that makes you...."

"Oh, a song like that," Walt jerked his thumb towards the speakers. "Yeah, we all do, don't we? I mean, there are things that will remind us of a person or place that'll just tear us apart inside. Every time I smell boiling potatoes, I think of my old man—he passed away ten years ago. I don't know why that makes me think of him still. I guess he liked potatoes, and my mom always had some cooking for him when he got home from work. It's kind of like what Proust wrote about in that book of his. You know, memory and how it works. How a simple smell or taste can bring back so much."

Walt became conscious of his hands again. He took a quick drink and brought both hands down to the stool which he then held onto like a small boy. The woman smiled at Walt, waiting, perhaps, to see if he would continue. But he just looked into his glass. After a minute, he looked up at her. She watched him closely.

They both began to speak at the same time.

"What's—"

"You go ahead," said Walt.

"I was just going to ask you what your name is."

"Simon," Walt said. "My name is Simon."

He held out his hand towards the woman.

"Nice to meet you, Simon. I'm Jane."

"Pleased to make your acquaintance, Jane."

"You were going to say something?"

Walt looked at her for a moment.

"Oh, I was just going to ask you what your name is."

They smiled at one another, and then laughed quietly. Walt looked out the window again. It was snowing, and he could see the roof of his car turning white under the snow, a pale disguise. From black to white.

Simple, he thought. There are things everywhere to remind us.

He looked at Jane.

"I had a family.... It's been over three years. They're far away, in another place. While I'm here in another place, yet."

Walt made this up as he went along. Maybe he thought it would help Jane forget about what had been troubling her. She looked at him sadly but said nothing.

"Now," Walt continued, "when I see a family, any family, I think of them. It's funny—I mean, every family is different. How does that book begin? 'All happy families are alike but each unhappy family is unhappy in its own way.' Maybe it's just the unhappy families I notice."

Jane's tears were gone. She smiled and looked out the window. People passed by; a few entered the bar and looked around. Some left, while others stayed and sat by themselves or joined others at tables around the room. The tables themselves were low and dimly lit. Smoke hovered thickly above the lights. The people in groups spoke loudly and laughed often. While at other tables, solitary people sat and quietly drank.

"It sounds like you read a lot. Are you a writer?" Jane asked.

"No. Just a reader. I work in a library."

"You're a librarian?"

"No, hell no. I do security and maintenance. I fix things up, make sure everything's running smoothly, stuff like that. But I still like to read. People think if you don't work right there in the books that you don't even know how to read." Walt looked at Jane and smiled. "I sure talk a lot, don't I? What do you do, Jane?"

"I'm an architect."

"No kidding. That's great. You build anything lately?"

"No. It's not as great as it sounds. Mostly I do a lot of the gopher work around the office. Paperwork, drawings of other people's work, running around. It's actually pretty boring."

"I would have thought it'd be a great job."

"Not yet. I'm just starting out."

Jane shrugged her shoulders and took another drink. She placed the glass gently down on the counter, ran her finger along the edge thoughtfully. Her lips parted slightly, as though she were about to speak, but she hesitated and took another drink.

"Where's your family?" She asked it quickly, and then covered her mouth with her hand. "I'm sorry. That's none of my business. You don't have to say."

"No. It's okay."

Walt looked at her openly. He let his hands rest, unselfconsciously—almost proudly—on the counter. His fingernails were dark and dirty.

"They're dead. They died in a car wreck over three years ago. It seems strange even now. I mean, to say it so bluntly. But at the same time it becomes easier to talk about. Not that it is ever easy." He took a deep breath and looked around the bar. "On my way in here tonight, I saw this guy asking for change. When he looked up at me to ask, I noticed one of his eyes was all scabbed and crusted shut. It looked infected and probably blind. Shit, I said, get yourself to a hospital. I gave him money for a cab. He said, 'Thanks, but I ain't got no health card. Thanks all the same.' And he turned and walked off with the money. But that's neither here nor there. I don't even know why I brought it up."

Jane listened intently. Both of their glasses were empty. She motioned over to the bartender. He was a thin man, with wire-rimmed glasses and the slightest hint of a beer belly forming under his button-up denim shirt. He wordlessly replaced both glasses with full ones and moved on to the next customer.

Walt did see that man asking for change outside. But telling Jane did not have the effect he hoped for. Immediately after his exchange with the man, Walt wanted to tell someone about him. He wanted to tell his wife, Karen; to describe to her what the man looked like, and what he said, how he said it. Walt often told her stories about the things he saw and heard and read. There was a time they could stay up all night talking, telling each other stories. But that was a long time ago.

Jane took a sip from her glass and spoke.

"This might sound weird, but I knew just looking at you that you had a story, a sad story. I mean, do you know how when you look in someone's eyes and you can just see that they have a sad, dark secret? A sadness in their eyes they can't hide—a heaviness that no matter how hard they try they just can't hide? I'm sorry. That sounds so stupid."

Walt looked surprised; he hadn't expected her to believe him so readily.

"Oh? No. I...I guess I just never really thought of it that way before."

"What happened? If you don't want to say, that's all right."

Walt became serious. He held his glass tightly with both hands.

"I was driving."

He looked up at Jane for her reaction. She was quiet, under-standing.

"We were on our way to Emma's—my wife's family's place for the weekend. There was Emma and our daughter, Lisa, and me. Lisa was six when.... It was snowing and just...bad, the weather was really bad. Like a blizzard or something. But I kept going. It wasn't far. I don't know. I guess I should've known."

"How could you have?"

"I don't know, I just...."

Walt had begun to believe his story. There was an accident, a minor one just a few days ago when he drove the car into a ditch. He and Karen were having an argument about something that Walt thought had no bearing on anything important. Until it turned suddenly, and Karen told him that she and Laura—their daughter who was asleep in the back seat—were leaving him. Karen accused Walt of being distant and withdrawn, of becoming another man, one who no longer cared for or about her. He had stopped loving her long ago, she said.

Walt was silent for a long time. He wanted to answer that it was she who had become distant and cold, uncaring. He wanted to say that he was leaving her for those same reasons. But when he opened his mouth to speak, the words were not there. So he considered pulling over. But when he turned and looked at Karen, lit only by the dashboard lights and the occasional headlights of passing cars, her face angry and confused—not unlike Walt's own face—his thoughts changed. He imagined kissing Karen and telling her that it was too important to throw away their marriage like that, they still had years and years left in them. Marriage, he wanted to say, is a sacred thing.

But what he blurted out was, "Is there someone else?"

Karen answered too quickly, "That's irrelevant."

Walt knew that meant yes, there was someone else. They were both quiet for a long time. And then Karen told him the truth. Once it was out in the open, Walt considered just forgetting about it and moving on from there. He tried to say what he had been thinking about saying earlier, about marriage and love. But then he pictured her with this anonymous man, imagined this man knowing secrets about his wife that he himself didn't know—and that was it. He couldn't control himself; he screamed, he shook his fists, he said things he had never before said to his wife. He pulled off the road too fast and drove the car into a ditch.

And for the first time in his life, Walt wanted to be dead.

Laura slept through the argument, the confession, the accident—everything. And Walt was thankful for that much. At least she was spared that stupidity. Because of the accident and because of everything, Walt decided to drop Laura and Karen off at his in-laws and then turn around and drive back home alone, to spend time drinking and figuring out what he would do. He had ominously hinted to Karen before driving off that it might be the last time she would see him—alive. He wanted her to feel bad, to regret everything she had said and done.

— • —

"What was she like?" Jane asked.

Walt was shaken from his reverie.

"My daughter?"

"Both of them."

"Emma was a nurse. She worked hard, took her job very seriously. She was a great mom, too. She was good at everything she did, once upon a time. Nice, kind, loving. There was nothing she couldn't do. She was a great wife. And Lisa was bright and quick and fun. It's hard not to think of what she might have become...."

Walt took a deep breath. That was how he wanted to remember Karen, but now everything was changed. He looked at Jane. Her expression was solemn, sympathetic. She looked as if she wanted to say something.

"The human spirit is vigorous," she said. "We can overcome so much."

"It's not easy, though."

"No. It's not easy."

They were both quiet. Snow continued to fall outside.

Walt didn't want to talk about it anymore. He was getting tired of the lie, and he wasn't sure he could keep it going any longer.

"I'm sorry for getting into this. I mean, the reason I came over here was to try and cheer you up, not to make you more depressed. What about you anyway? What's your story? You have a boyfriend?"

"He's getting married tomorrow."

Walt raised his eyebrows.

"We broke up about five months ago. Now he's getting married to someone he just met. We were together almost seven years, and not once did he mention marriage. They haven't even been together three months. I really shouldn't care, but I do. Anyway, now I'm here trying to forget about it.... I'm sorry. This is probably boring you."

"No. Of course not. But I certainly asked the wrong question, didn't I? We're a couple of downers. Have you spoken to him?"

"No. He didn't even call to tell me. I had to hear it from someone else." Jane tried to smile but ended up just shrugging her shoulders. "You know, I've never been to a bar by myself before. I guess it took this kind of thing to get me here. I worry that's it. I'll probably never leave this place." She smiled and held up her glass. "A toast to drowning our sorrows."

"To drowning our sorrows."

They both tilted their heads back and took long drinks, looking over their glasses at each other and smiling with their eyes.

Cars drove past outside. It was cold, but not so cold that people walked by bundled up with parkas and hoods and scarves. Some walked by wearing thin fall jackets. While others, the young men and women on their way to noisy, crowded bars and clubs, strode by in long sleeved shirts, hatless and, perhaps, a little remorseful. The women were visibly shivering, wrapping their arms around themselves, and the men, some wearing only jeans and tight t-shirts, were acting as though it was already summer. Jane pointed outside to the snow, ignoring the passersby.

"Looks like Christmas all over again."

"Look at those fools," Walt said.

"Yeah. I used to be one of those fools. But that was a long time ago."

They laughed though neither knew why. Perhaps, it was the effect of the alcohol slowly making its way to their heads, pulsing its way up and around. The room had yet to begin spinning. It was not that kind of night. It only gave them a pleasant feeling of warmth and comfort along with the freedom to forget about certain things, for a certain time.

"I bet you were a great father."

"Yes.... No. It's hard to say. I mean, I worked a lot. I guess I could have been around more. It's easy to think things would be different now."

Walt turned quiet, thoughtful. He pointed to the window.

"All those people are leaving. They're leaving homes and families and friends. Eventually everyone leaves. Like your boyfriend. Like my dad…just like my family. Before the accident, Emma and I were arguing about something. It doesn't matter what it was about now. Some silly little thing. But at that moment, I was thinking about leaving, too. In some ways our marriage had been over for a long time. It was no longer the most important thing in either of our lives. When I think about it now, I think I must have been crazy. What I'd give to have them both back."

Walt drained his glass. He thought that by reversing who was leaving whom, he could actually turn it around somehow, that he could convince himself that it was his idea to leave her. Or that

Karen was calling him at home now, unable to sleep because she wanted a second chance.

"What did you do? After the accident?" Jane asked, tilting her head to the side so that she had to look up at Walt.

"Oh, I guess I drank a little more than usual. Tried not to think about it. But every night, while I slept, there they were in my dreams."

He was speaking now of Karen and her lover. He couldn't get them out of his mind.

"That's so sad. I'm sorry." Jane held out her hand but quickly pulled it back.

"Yeah."

She looked into Walt's eyes.

"Do you mind if I ask why you were thinking of leaving them?"

"No. That's fair. I guess I just felt like I wanted to be the first to go. Not to die, but just to go. I knew it couldn't last forever."

"But isn't marriage supposed to be forever?"

"That's what I thought."

Jane appeared to consider this. She looked around the bar at the other people sitting in there. The other people with families and friends and places to go, places to leave.

"You don't have to answer this if you don't want to," Jane began, "but why do you think it's so easy for men to leave? I mean, my dad left. I know other people whose dads left. My boyfriend, he just left. What the hell's the matter with us women, anyway?"

She tried to smile but she was serious—and a little drunk.

"Women leave, too," Walt said.

"Yes, they do. But not as often as men. Am I right?"

"I wouldn't know." Walt tilted his glass back to get the last drop and then noisily placed it down on the counter. "I should go," he said.

Jane laughed and pointed to her glass.

"I'm sorry. That was the beer talking. Not me. Please, have another drink. It's on me. I don't want to go home yet."

Walt looked at her for a moment and then nodded. Jane motioned to the bartender.

"Two more, please. You haven't heard my theory yet," she said to Walt. "You want to know what I think?"

"Yeah, sure."

Walt settled onto his stool, resting his elbows on the counter. It was well after midnight. Karen was probably asleep now, in the same bed she slept in as a child.

"Okay. Here's how I see it. The men are all leaving because...."

Jane got quiet. She placed a finger over her lips and looked around the room to see if anyone was listening to her. No one was. The few remaining people in the bar were busy talking or listening to the music or watching the silenced TV. Walt looked around the room as well. He let his eyes rest on the TV above Jane's head for a moment. There were talking heads without voices. The sound was turned down to allow for the music on the stereo. If one were to look quickly at the TV and then away, it might have appeared that the news was really a music video, and that nothing that was actually happening was real.

The bartender changed the channel.

Jane spoke in a hushed tone.

"Men are afraid and restless and bored and unable to make meaningful connections with other human beings because they have no sense of place, no sense of duty. You're all rootless—deracinated." She said this last word as though she were spelling it at the same time; slowly, carefully, and weighing it for value. She continued. "You can just keep moving on, not putting down any roots. Whenever the hell you want. No matter how many kids you have, or how many wives. You all just leave. Because you can. Women can leave, too, but we hardly ever do. Someone has to stay home and look after the kids. We have that sense of home. We work at things like relationships and sticking together, and making our families happy. While you guys work at golf."

Walt stared at his hands and picked at the dirt under his fingernails. He was listening to her speak but he didn't believe a word. He looked up.

"I hate golf," he said.

"I guess I sound like a real bitch. I'm just a little bitter if you haven't noticed. I'm sorry, it's not really fair to say that to you now. I'm such an idiot."

She looked at him and smiled, and then turned quiet. Walt was not quite sure what to say about any of it.

"Listen, I—" Walt stopped and looked up at the clock.

"What? Are you going to turn into a pumpkin?" Jane laughed.

"Yeah. I better go. I'm sorry."

"Why are you sorry?"

"For…for bringing all that up. For telling you all that."

"Don't be sorry. We're just two strangers in a bar."

"Yeah, two strange people in a bar."

They both laughed, and for a moment Walt thought he could go home with Jane. It was to be a night of quiet revenge. He looked at Jane in that way, as one who is considering going home with a stranger. And Jane returned his look. They were both quiet and—for just a second—sober. Walt imagined undressing Jane in a near-dark room lit only by a streetlight outside the window. He wondered what it would be like to be with another woman after all these years.

He leaned in towards her. And they kissed. They were drunk once more.

Jane ended the kiss and smiled.

"You know," she said, "when I came here tonight, I thought I'd pick up some guy and sleep with him and forget his name by morning. That's what I came here for. Not heavy conversation. Not to find a therapist. Just to meet some guy and lose myself for a night. To pretend that I was someone else. Because I didn't want to be me. You ever feel like that? Have you ever just wanted to be someone else?"

"Yeah. I guess I have."

Walt was surprised by her frankness, by her intentions that were not unlike his own. He looked at Jane differently. He also looked around the room at the other women there, women he imagined to be less complicated than Jane.

"I was sure I could do it. Just come in here, meet a guy and.... Well, that's just not me. You know? You can only pretend so much and then it catches up. I'm not an actress. Sometimes I wish I were. If this were a movie, maybe we'd live happily ever after."

Walt laughed.

"Unless it was a French movie," he said. "Then one of us would commit suicide or get hit by a car."

"Sounds like fun."

Walt sighed.

"I have a confession to make," he said.

"Ohhhh." Jane laughed and spun herself around on the stool. "Save it. I mean for a minute. I have to go to the bathroom."

She got up and walked unsteadily to the back of the bar. The bartender cleared empty glasses from the tables, emptied ashtrays. Walt watched the TV. A woman in a skin-tight jump suit and a ten gallon hat was dancing and singing on a stage in front of thousands of people.

The bar was emptying out. People were gathering their coats and throwing cash onto tables. They shuffled across the floor, hesitant and anxious. Cabs waited outside. Some people, who were in no shape to drive, fumbled in their pockets for keys or money. The music was turned off. The volume on the TV was turned up, the channel was changed. Walt looked up. The news was on again. A plane had crashed into the Atlantic ocean. He had seen the footage half a dozen times already today, but this was the first time he heard the commentary. There were many dead. And no chance of finding survivors.

Jane believed Walt's wife was dead. And his daughter. And that he, Walt, was the survivor. But he didn't feel like a survivor. Not anymore. And they were not dead but just asleep a few hundred kilometres away. And maybe his wife was feeling remorseful, and having a guilty, restless sleep in her parents' home with her daughter there, too—a reminder for them both.

Jane returned. She looked around the bar at the few remaining people. They were all preparing to leave.

"I guess we ought to go." She smiled at Walt, drunkenly. "Do you want to come over for a coffee?"

Walt smiled.

"No, thank you, really. I should just go home. It's late and I work early tomorrow."

"Yeah, of course. I'm sorry I—"

"No, don't be sorry. Thanks for asking. Maybe another time."

"Yeah. Another time."

Jane put some money down on the counter and took her coat off the stool next to her. Walt counted out a couple of bills and placed them under a not quite finished glass of beer.

"You said you had a confession."

"Oh, that. No, it's nothing."

Jane zipped up her coat and followed Walt to the door. They stepped outside into the cold night air. The snow was still falling. It was quiet, everything was hushed and white. From the ground up, whiteness. Jane stopped and turned to Walt.

"Hey, is Simon your real name?"

"No. I guess it's not. Is Jane yours?"

"No."

Walt smiled and watched Jane walk away through the snow. He just watched her walk away. It was a big city and chances were he would never see her again. He went over to his car and pushed the snow off the windshield with the sleeve of his coat. But snow continued to fall covering the windshield as soon as he brushed it away. The sky was light in the way the night sky is light only in the winter, reflecting the whiteness of the snow below it, the snow all around. He closed his eyes and stood there for a long time with the tip of his tongue catching snowflakes, cool for only a split second, warmed and melted by his breath. He felt happy for a moment, like a child tasting snow for the first time. Everything else melted away. And then he felt bad about things turning out like this, and he felt bad about telling Jane that his family was dead. He cleared the windshield one last time and then got into his car and drove home through the falling snow.

DRINKING

This happened back when I was still with my wife, Liz, back when we were still a family living together in a small apartment on the wrong side of the tracks, so to speak. We were just starting out, but already we had two kids, and too many debts and troubles to mention. We had a hard time just making ends meet, and we didn't always get along very well. But we pretended like everything was fine and good—you know, for the kids, for the neighbours. I was drinking a little more than I should have been, and Liz was working hard to keep us all afloat. That's not to say I wasn't working, because I was. I did different jobs, anything I could get. But then something would always happen to get me canned. And I'd be back where I started.

Across the street from the walk-up we lived in then was a modest high-rise, maybe twelve stories high. It blocked out the sun for us most of the time, which was symbolic of something in those days. And it didn't make for much of a view: concrete and windows, nothing much else. Sometimes at night, though, Liz and I would turn out the lights after the kids had gone to bed and just watch the people over there. They were always coming and going. We'd watch them living their lives, as we imagined they probably did with us. We'd see old ladies watering their plants on their balconies, or the big hairy man that came out to check the weather with just a towel wrapped around him. This always cracked us up. We'd make up stories about them all, imagine what their lives were like, what they did for a living. It's strange, but this was a good time for us, a time when everything else slipped away and we just enjoyed each other's company: Liz and I sitting in the dark by the window, with drinks in our hands, watching and making up hard luck stories worse than our own. We didn't have a TV back then, so I guess this was our entertainment. It was usually pretty quiet over there; not much outside of the ordinary ever happened.

After we had been there for a while things started turning sour between Liz and me—and it became futile to make like everything was fine. We were both hot-headed and hard to live with in those days. And then there was my daydreaming, this idea I had of striking out on my own to write a novel. That probably made me even harder to live with. But then things would pick up; we'd get some money or some good luck, and everything would be fine for a few weeks or even months. But like the ebb and flow of a body of water, our luck would inevitably turn and head back out to sea.

One night Liz and I were going at it, saying things you'd never imagine saying to your husband or wife. After a while all kinds of stuff started coming up to the surface, things I'd long since thought were forgotten. We dredged up past lies and secrets, small infidelities from before we were married—a drunken kiss at a party, or the way I looked at the woman living downstairs from us then—anything we could get our hands or memories on.

Liz said, "You only married me because I was pregnant."

I said, "Maybe I did. But you only got pregnant because you wanted me to marry you."

Another thing she said was, "You live in the future, always scheming and planning, and waiting for the getaway car. Always making plans for something that won't ever happen. Just give it up," she said. "You think you'll be this big time writer when you haven't even written a word yet. You can barely spell. You're never going to be that person, Will. You're just going to be you: a poor, lazy dope with no prospects, no future."

Oh, it went on and on. Hateful things that may have been true or may have been false. But that wasn't the point. I stood there and listened. I wondered how long she had had these thoughts. There wasn't much I could say. I shook my head.

"Do you hate me that much?" I asked.

She looked at me and I looked at her. We were both quiet.

It was almost a relief when we heard the electric guitar start up. Liz and I turned from one another and looked out the window. A song would start, maybe the first few bars, and then it would stop. Then squealing guitar sounds and another song would start. It was loud, and I mean really loud. We figured it was coming from the place across the street, from one of the balconies. The sound carried, came right into our place and sent the windows vibrating. We could hear people yelling at whoever it was making this noise, telling him to turn it down—but no, I guess he couldn't hear them, and it continued.

I cranked our stereo right up. You know, to drown it out, maybe get the message across that way, but our neighbours only complained and thought I was the one being a nuisance, which I guess I was.

This went on for a while and then it stopped. Liz and I were too worn out to keep up with our row, so we went to sleep after that; her in the bed and me on the couch. But the next night, the noise started up again. By that time Liz and I were barely speaking to each other. It's amazing how much you can communicate with a look, a gesture. We managed to get through the entire day exchanging not much more than five or six words. Instead, we'd talk to the kids, get little jabs in at each other through them. "Let's get you cleaned up for bed," Liz would say, "because God knows your father is too concerned about his own sorry self to worry about a petty thing like your well being." I was no better. I know, it sounds terrible using them like that, but they were too young to really understand. Liz and I were being childish—no, not even childish because the kids would never have done something like that. We were just being mean, defensive and mean.

On that second night the racket got so bad I had to do something. The kids were in bed, but they couldn't get to sleep. At first, they sang and sang in their shaky kid voices as loud as they could, to try and ignore it the way they did when Liz and I were fighting: "You are my sunshine, my only sunshine...." But it was too loud. And at one point they were both crying, calling to me, "Please, daddy, make it stop." Then, to make matters worse, Liz and I were fighting again, or still. We'd decided to start talking to each other, but only to argue. I don't even remember what it was about at that point. Every conversation, every argument eventually blurred into the next: over bills, drinking, my other bad habits, my as-yet-unwritten novel. I started to blame the electric guitar; I believed that if it hadn't started up, if it hadn't continued, we could sit, Liz and I, and talk things out like two adults. Instead, we screamed over the noise, calling each other names.

Liz slammed the bathroom door shut and ran the water in there to drown out the noise. I decided to go outside and get some air. The racket was even worse out there. They could probably hear it down the block. It was blaring. That's when I decided to go pay the guy a visit. I'd had it. I didn't know what I was going to say, but it couldn't go on like that. I'd tell him it was tearing apart my marriage, driving my kids to tears. I didn't care what I told him, just so long as it stopped.

I went into the building and walked up the stairs. It wasn't hard to find his place, I could have closed my eyes and found it in no time. I could hear other people yelling at the guy. Things like, "Shut the fuck up." And, "Turn that shit down." I knocked on the door and then gave it a kick. There was no way he was going to hear me with that guitar going. After banging a little harder, I tried the handle; the door was unlocked. I waited another second and then let myself in. The place was dark and kind of creepy. But the noise was not as loud in there as I had expected. I walked down the hall and into what was the living room. And there was this guy, naked, sitting on his couch playing an electric guitar. His head hung down as he played, so he didn't see me at first. The cable from his guitar stretched across the floor and out onto the balcony. Another cable, the one I was looking for, reached across the room from the balcony and was plugged into the wall to my left. I walked over and yanked the cord out.

The noise stopped and it was quiet. I took a deep breath.

The guy looked up at me. He didn't have much of a reaction. He was probably in his thirties; a bit flabby, with long dirty hair. He just looked up at me and kind of smiled.

"Listen buddy," I said to him, "this has got to stop. It's too damn loud. Christ, you're keeping up the whole neighbourhood."

He didn't say anything. Just looked at me with these big watery eyes.

"I mean it, pal. It's tearing apart my marriage. The kids can't sleep. They're crying over there—I live across the goddamn street—and they're crying over there. And the wife's just taking it out on me. Buy some headphones or something. Just don't play it so loud."

"You want a cookie?"

"Do I want a cookie? No, I don't want a goddamn cookie. What I want is for you to turn down your damn amplifier."

"My wife made 'em. They're real good." He put the guitar aside and stood up. He scratched himself and looked around. I spotted an old tattered housecoat on the chair next to me. I handed it to him.

"Thanks," he said. He put on the housecoat, tied it up and walked out of the room.

I could not believe that this man had a wife, that someone would actually marry a man like him. I wondered where the hell the wife was. I looked around the room; it was tiny. There was a couch, a chair, a stereo and a TV. That was about it. The TV was on and some game show was playing. Someone had just won a car. After a minute, the guy came back out carrying a glass of milk in one hand and a little chipped ceramic plate with some cookies on it in the other. One look at the cookies and I knew his wife didn't make them. Somebody's wife may have made them. In a factory somewhere. They were those store bought variety, chocolate chip, perfectly round and hard as a rock.

"Your wife made these?" I asked skeptically.

"Yeah," he said.

He put the plate down on the floor where a coffee table would have been and sat down.

He then bit into a cookie.

"Sorry," he said, indicating the glass of milk in his hand. "No more milk."

I reached down and got myself a cookie.

"Where's your wife?" I asked, looking around. It was the kind of place where you wouldn't be entirely surprised to find the wife chopped up in the freezer.

He looked at me for a moment as if he was trying to remember.

"Gone," he said.

"Gone," I repeated. I nodded my head. A real nut case, this one. "Okay, so listen. We understand one another?"

He looked up at me with a blank expression, like he didn't know if I was talking to him or to someone else in there. He was definitely out of it. I probably could have asked him who the prime minister was and he wouldn't have known.

"That...music you're playing: Keep it down. Got it. Otherwise, I come back and toss that thing off the balcony." I pointed towards the amplifier.

"Sit down," he said. He didn't appear to have heard a word I said.

I had no idea what I was dealing with. The guy had obviously lost it, or never had it to begin with. But I sat down. Something— I don't know what, maybe because I didn't want to go home just then—but something kept me there. It was kind of interesting to watch the guy. I was waiting for him to say something, maybe give me some clues regarding his life, or where his wife was, or about any of it.

"You smoke?" he asked.

I was about to say yes, but I saw that he was pulling a joint out of the pocket of his housecoat and smoothing out the ends with his mouth.

"No. Not anymore. Tell me, why do you figure you have to play your guitar so loud, anyway? And why the hell is that thing out on the balcony? I mean, most people, they just turn it up so they can hear it, not so the whole goddamn city can hear it."

He lit the joint and slowly inhaled.

"Dunno."

"Maybe you should join a band or something. You know, to get this out of your system in a controlled environment. Maybe play with some buddies in a basement or garage somewhere. Preferably on the other side of town."

Again, he looked at me with that big blank face like a moon.

"Listen," I said. "Just keep it down, okay?"

He didn't say anything. He tried to blow smoke rings into the air, but they came out as thin, wispy clouds.

"Okay then," I said, standing up to go.

"Wife's been gone for sometime now. Took just about everything with her."

I looked at him and around the apartment. Like I said, there wasn't much in there.

"That's too bad," I said. "Maybe if you didn't play your music so loud she'd come back."

It was a low blow, but what the hell. The guy was so out there I'm sure he didn't hear what I said. He watched me but didn't say anything else. So I walked out and closed the door behind me. I stood out in the hall a minute and waited to see if he'd start it back up again. Just as I was about to walk away, it did start up. And this time it was ear shattering feedback I heard. It was painful. I was about to go back in and give him a piece of my mind, but he turned it right off.

I found my way out.

The sky was black, and the moon was out, silver and round. It was a beautiful night, and I thought about walking around for a while, maybe going out for a drink. I looked across the street and saw Liz up in our kitchen window. She was doing the dishes and gazing up at the moon. I wondered—if I was seeing her for the first time, would I think she was the kind of woman I'd want to marry? Was she the kind of woman that could make me happy? The more I looked, the more I thought, yes, yes she is. With the light behind her and her head tilted up towards the moon, she did look beautiful, there was no doubt about that. But being on the outside looking in did make me think about things in a different way. Not bad, but not exactly good either. Just different.

Sometimes it seemed like too many hurdles had presented themselves to us, and we couldn't get over them all, not the way we were going. We kept getting tripped up. It's crazy to think about it now because so much has changed. But then, in other important ways, nothing has changed. I'm still the fool I was then; and Liz and the kids—God bless them—are still the same people they were. The only thing is, we're all older now, and supposedly wiser.

I went back in and told Liz what had happened, said what a stoner the guy was. And I said that if it happened again I was going to throw his amplifier off the balcony. Liz laughed about that, so I made up some other things, embellished the story a little. It's funny, the things you say when you're mad. Or scared. Liz and I didn't fight any more that night. After she was done with the dishes, I poured us each a rum and Coke, and shut off the lights.

"Do you want to watch the neighbours?" she asked.

"No. Let's just sit."

So we sat there with our drinks and we talked. It was the first time in ages that we just talked. We talked about the guy across the street and his hard luck story. We felt bad for him in a way. But that was life, Liz said. We also talked about the future and about the past. And we talked about the kids and what we thought they might do with their lives. We talked and talked until we were too tired to talk anymore. And then we just sat there in the dark and the quiet, and we both kind of turned our chairs and looked out the window. Most of the lights were out across the street, and it was quiet, too. Before long, we decided to turn in for the night—and went to bed.

I didn't hear that guy's music again until the day I moved out. Liz and the kids were staying there, without me, for a while. It's a long story, and one I'd rather not go into. I'll only say that it was my idea to leave. I loaded the truck up with some of my stuff. Not much: some clothes, my books and a few other odds and ends. I didn't want to take too much. I was leaving them with enough of a hole in their lives as it was. Anyway, that's when I heard the electric guitar. I was putting a box in the back of the truck when it started up. I looked up towards his balcony— the sound was louder than ever—and there he was. He could have been naked, but I could only see him from the waist up because of the concrete balcony and the guitar he had strapped on. He waved down at me and I waved back. Then he just stood there playing his guitar and watching me, the sound blaring, until I drove off twenty minutes later.

A BEAUTIFUL DAY FOR A
FUNERAL

A fter waiting for well over an hour, the minister sat down on the church steps and absently skimmed over the words of chapter six of the Song of Solomon. His thin finger traced an invisible line across the page as though smoothing it out, flattening it. The passage had been chosen by the bride and groom to be read during the ceremony. *Whither is thy beloved gone....* The sun glared off the clean white page, causing the minister to squint his eyes until he could no longer read what was printed there. He took off his glasses and rubbed at his eyes for a long time. He had never seen anything like it.

The minister had met the bride only once, at the rehearsal just days before. She had appeared warm and loving towards the young groom—whispering into his ear and then giggling, and placing small kisses on his cheek while they went through the various aspects of the ceremony. She brought the sound of laughter to a room that was otherwise serious—even tense, the minister observed. Her parents had argued then just as they did now—inside the church, and only a few feet away from where the minister sat on the steps. They had argued about the choice of flowers and music, the caterers and the food. And they had even argued, the minister noted, about the distance they had to travel to get to the wedding. The minister could hear them now, their voices angry and annoyed—and confused. And he could smell the bride's father's cigar. Once already the minister had asked him not to smoke inside the church, and the man had apologized, butting out the cigar on the bottom of his shoe and then placing it in his coat pocket.

Closing his bible, the minister rose slowly and stood outside the church doors looking in. Earlier, one of the groom's brothers had stood in the same place asking the guests, "Bride or groom?" and then directing them to the correct side of the small church. It made little difference now.

— • —

The bride's parents had remained inside the church all this time; ceaselessly arguing, their voices rising and falling as though they were not arguing at all, but instead passionately singing an operatic score. They were to wait and walk their daughter—together, as a family—down the aisle. Now they could not agree on whose daughter she was. ("Your daughter," said the father bluntly, "is not late: she's not coming. She can't be late if she's not coming. It's illogical.") Nor could they decide whether they should stay or call it a day and drive, in their separate cars, the six hundred kilometers to their separate homes.

"She's not showing," said the father. "I'm not going to wait here for someone who isn't ever going to arrive."

"Well, I'm not leaving until I hear some kind of explanation," said the mother. "She wouldn't just disappear like that."

"Don't be so damn stubborn. You know as well as I do that she's not coming." The father examined his cigar.

"What kind of thing is that to say? You act as if you knew this was going to happen."

"Let's just say," said the father looking up from his cigar, "I'm not at all surprised. You know what kind of girl she is. And who knows what kind of kid he is." He indicated over his shoulder with his thumb to where he imagined the groom to be sitting.

On and on they went, lowering their voices when they thought they heard someone outside the church—the rustling pages of the minister's Bible; footsteps at the entrance—and then raising them again when they got too upset to consider those outside. Upon seeing the minister enter the church, the bride's father looked quickly down at the cigar in his hand and then back to the minister again. He shrugged his shoulders, making an apologetic bow, and leaned down to butt out the cigar on the sole of his shoe.

The bride's mother shook her head disapprovingly and looked out the window to where the guests stood waiting.

— • —

Outside, the guests were getting restless. They milled about on the grass, making small talk and referring to the *situation* in hushed tones. Some were still expecting to see the bride's car come around the corner and drive into the parking lot where she would finally emerge, looking both lovely and innocent in her white dress, and with some excuse on her lips. Others were waiting for someone else to leave first, so they would not have to be the one to do so, to be the first to give up. Every now and then, each guest in turn would stop chattering long enough to glance up to the top of the hill behind the church to where the groom sat alone in the grass. They would shake their heads slowly and sympathetically and then turn back to their laboured conversations.

There was still no sign of the young bride.

When she was just fifteen minutes late, someone suggested that there could have been an accident along the way. There just had to be an explanation. Others agreed. "Yes, yes," they murmured. "An accident. Oh my, what an inauspicious beginning. I hope it's not serious." It was decided—after unanswered calls were made— that someone drive to town, following the route the bride and her maid of honour would have driven. The groom had been present for all of this. "Maid of honour," he muttered sarcastically, though no one heard him. He put his hand in his pocket and clutched a small piece of paper he had found pushed under his door that morning. But he remained quiet as the search party left the parking lot. And before the car was even out of sight—while some of the children still ran along side the car, waving and calling out "Good luck"—the groom turned and walked up the hill behind the church. It wasn't long before the search party returned without the bride.

As for the best man, he was now sitting in his car smoking a joint and listening to the radio. He had done his best to assure everyone that the bride would be arriving at any moment. He tried to explain that this was not unusual for her, not at all surprising. She was always a little late. Late even for their first date—just over a year ago. Everyone laughed when he told them this, and it made him feel like he was doing his job. But though no one said so, it quickly became apparent to most of the people there that she was not coming, not then and not later. That's when the best man got into his car and loosened his tie.

— • —

It was quiet on the hill. A few of the children continued to play next to the road, occasionally yelling "Car car car," followed by the inevitable "False alarm!" or "It's not them!" The groom sat there still. He had ignored the efforts of his best man, and those of his mother, both of whom had more than once used the expression:

"You're too good for her, anyway." And now the groom's mother stood at the bottom of the hill barring anyone from going up to speak with him. "He made it clear," she repeated, "that he'd like to be alone." Just how he made that clear, she did not say.

Overhead, an eagle gracefully ascended into the pale blue sky. Round and round it spiraled, gaining altitude with each revolution. It reminded the groom of a poem he had once read in school. Something about things falling apart, the center not holding. But that was all he could remember. He sat there in his suit and looked down at his polished shoes, his black socks. The way he sat caused the cuffs of his pants to rise half way up his shins, thus appearing far too short for him. And his socks slouched down towards his pale ankles. He pulled up his socks deliberately and straightened out his legs. His suit felt tight, and hot. He loosened his tie, and unbuttoned his jacket. He pushed the hair from his eyes and looked down the hill to where his father stood. The older man inhaled from his cigarette and looked up and down the gravel road.

Dust rose above the road less than half a kilometer away. The groom could see this from where he sat at the top of the hill. It had not rained in days and the roads were very dry. The dust was high above the trees, hovering briefly and then beginning a slow descent. There was a trail of it leading towards the church, rising and falling. Before long, a car came into view, speeding down the road and kicking up dust in its wake. The groom watched his father throw a cigarette into the road and begin to light another as the unfamiliar car continued past and out of sight.

He lay back in the grass and gazed up at the sky. Clouds sailed by overhead; the wind picked up. As a boy, he sat on this very hill and watched the clouds above, trying to will them to disappear. It was a trick he learned from a book, but never actually mastered.

The noise of the children playing next to the road receded, drifting away like the clouds. And here he was on the hill again, but with his family and friends, and people he only vaguely recognized—all waiting for him. Or rather, waiting for his betrothed....

He sat back up and looked at all the guests at the bottom of the hill. They had all been watching him in turn, and whispering. He looked from face to face, and, as with the clouds, he tried to make them disappear simply by willing them to. His mother was among them attempting to reassure everyone that everything would be all right. She patted the backs of some and hugged others, nodding her head and smiling the whole time. And when she turned and saw the groom looking down at her, the smile slowly left her face, and she just stared up at him sadly, and he knew what she was thinking, and what she would do next.

— • —

"You'll get your pants dirty," she said, slightly out of breath from climbing to the top of the small hill.

He looked up at her with a vacant expression. His mother waited for him to speak, but he didn't, so she spoke again.

"I don't know what to say. I told you—"

"Jesus Christ, Mom, please."

His mother looked around nervously.

"The minister is too close to be talking like that."

"The last thing I need to hear right now is I told you so."

"I'm just saying—"

"I know what you're saying and I don't want to hear it."

"Listen. This is going to be okay. You'll see. There's no point in us arguing. And there's no sense in you sitting here all day getting your pants dirty."

"I don't give a damn about my pants."

The groom threw a handful of grass and dirt at his mother's feet. It crumbled before her, and bits of grass and dirt landed on her clean red shoes. She looked down at her shoes and then at her son.

"I'm sorry," he said. "I know you mean well but.... Please just do me a favour and tell everyone to go home. I'm sorry."

"Don't be sorry. You're the last person who should be saying that. If anyone should be sorry, it's—"

"Shut up." He clenched his teeth. "Please. Just stop."

She bit her lower lip. But she wasn't done.

"You haven't done anything wrong. This is not about you. It's about her. It's her thing. She's just got cold feet, is all. Now, will you please stand up and walk down there with me?"

"No—"

"Your father is worried about you."

He looked down the hill to where his father stood, smoking and kicking at the gravel by the side of the road.

"It's over," he said, still watching his father. "She's not coming. Send everybody home."

"What do you mean? She's not coming at all?"

He looked up at his mother.

"She's not coming. The search party is back. And she's still not her. She left a letter under my door. I found it this morning."

His mother appeared confused. She looked at him blankly.

"But why didn't you say something? Why didn't you tell—"

"What was I supposed to say? Please just tell them to go. She's not coming. Tell them it's canceled. It's over."

He pointed to some of the guests who were huddled in a small group, smoking and talking and looking up at him.

"But...but...the food, the cake—"

"Just tell them. Please, Mother. Just do that for me."

His mother stood there with her mouth open, speechless. She continued to stare at him, waiting for a punchline, or for him to say he was kidding. She looked around, at the bushes and trees, as though expecting the bride to jump out and say "Surprise!" or "You're on Candid Camera." But there was no one there. And the groom remained quiet, staring at her, and then past her to the bottom of the hill where his father was looking out across the road. Behind him were the guests. Some paced back and forth impatiently, now, repeatedly looking at their watches. Others appeared to be waiting their turn to come speak with him. Waiting to give him their condolences.

"It's like a funeral," he whispered, looking down at the guests.

Tears slowly filled his mother's eyes.

"But why?" she implored, kneeling down to face him.

He said nothing. And his mother leaned in and kissed him softly on the cheek. She then stood up, composed herself and straightened out her dress.

"It's for the best, honey," she said, brushing a blade of grass from her dress. She turned and quickly walked away.

He wanted to pick up another clump of grass and throw it at her, but instead he just watched her go. She carefully walked down the steep slope towards the guests. The heels of her shoes dug into the grass leaving a trail of small holes on the hillside. The sun beat down.

It was becoming more and more like a funeral every minute.

— • —

One of the women standing in the grass approached his mother as she descended the hill. The woman reached up—she was a short, round woman—and put her arm around his mother's shoulders. Standing on her tip-toes, she whispered something in his mother's ear. And then gave her a hug. Other women approached and formed a circle. They would occasionally look up at him sitting there. One of them would say something, and the rest would shake their heads sadly before turning back into the circle. The minister, still carrying his Bible, joined the circle, too. They spoke for some time like that.

The minister finally broke the circle and walked quickly back to the church. He stopped at the top of the stairs and turned to face the guests, who were all watching and waiting. The group of women at the bottom of the hill stopped talking and watched the minister, as well. From where he sat, the groom could see the minister's mouth moving, but he could not hear what the minister was saying; he could only guess. After he finished speaking, the minister nodded his head solemnly and walked into the church. The groom's mother and the other women exchanged a few more words, and then their small procession made its way across the grass to the parked cars.

His father flicked another cigarette into the road and kicked softly at the gravel.

— • —

People started leaving. The first to go did so sheepishly, looking at their watches and nodding obscurely to the groom's parents or to the bride's parents, who had decided to wait after all, and who, finally, had appeared from the cloister of the church, though still bickering. The guests got into their parked cars, started the engines, fastened their seatbelts. They took their time, as if by stalling they were somehow giving the bride one last chance to appear. But one by one, people left. They were all too uncertain of what they should say to the groom, so they simply waved or pretended he was not there.

The groom sat alone watching the last guests leave. The small balloons his sister had tied to the trees by the road were blowing wildly in the wind and bouncing off the trees. One lone balloon fell to the ground and blew down the road like a tumbleweed. A few more cars pulled away. He considered going down there and shaking hands with the last of the guests, assuring them that he would be okay, that he'd get over this soon, real soon. But like the clouds overhead, the feeling passed.

His mother, who had been watching him, turned away. She walked over to where his father leaned against the fender of their car and stood next to him. He had a cigarette in his mouth, which she plucked out and inhaled from. She hadn't smoked in over ten years. She leaned her head back and blew smoke into the air, and then left her head like that, looking up at the sky.

The groom stood up and brushed himself off. Looking down the hill at the church he attended as a boy, he noticed how small it seemed. And how small the hill and his parents appeared from up there. How small it had all become. He reached into his pocket and took out the piece of paper he had found pushed under his door that morning. It was creased and warm from being in his pocket all afternoon. He began to unfold it but stopped and read only the words he could see, *love* and *sorry*. And the words *please forgive me.* He crumpled it up and let it fall to the ground.

Slowly, and with his hands in his pockets, the groom followed the trail of small holes in the ground that led to his mother and her high-heeled shoes, and to his father who stood next to her, lighting another cigarette and watching him make his way down the hill towards them.

EVERYTHING AS IT SHOULD BE

K ate woke up with her arms around the Sobey's bag boy. The first thing she saw was the back of the boy's neck, muscular and tanned. She turned just so, to look at his ear. It was pink, perfect. Short, translucent hairs covered the flawless ear, little hairs that were soft to the touch. Kate rubbed them one way and then the other. She had a thing for ears. She let her fingers linger and then glide from the boy's ear to his neck, along his back and down, down.

The boy continued to sleep as the room grew brighter. A large bay window looked out onto the street. Kate had left the curtains open since they were like that when she arrived at the house. She was accustomed to living in other people's houses as though she were some kind of phantom house-sitter. Before bringing home the bag boy, she had been sleeping on top of the bed covers in her sleeping bag. But then the boy came along, and Kate whipped off the blankets and they slept between the cool sheets. The light from the streetlight poured in over them in the night; it was soft and warm like a feather duvet. And the way it illuminated the boy's skin. Kate closed her eyes and cuddled in close to the bag boy. *Oh, that light....* She envisioned the square of light that lit up his chest. And the thin blond hair that fell across his eyes. His cheeks that were rosy and hot.

He called himself Cal. He was only eighteen.

Kate had gone for a walk to the all-night grocery store the night before. She was having trouble sleeping and wanted to get out, without *going out*. The store was brightly lit but nearly empty. A few shoppers straggled up and down the aisles in a sleepy daze. It was half past eleven. Kate picked up a sliced honeydew melon filled with grapes and covered in clear wrap. After examining it for a moment, she carried it over to the coffee shop at the back of the store. The coffee shop was closed and there was no one around. So Kate got a plastic spoon and unwrapped the melon. She hadn't intended to eat it without paying; her mind was on other things.

Since arriving in Halifax in the fall, Kate had been at odds with herself: thinking about staying, thinking about going. She felt like she was at a crossroads in her life; things were about to change, she was about to change, though she didn't know how or why or when. So when Cal walked over after a while and sat across from Kate at the small round table, she saw in him some kind of sign or omen. He had on his store uniform: green pants and a white short-sleeved button down. His hair was parted to the side, covering one of his perfect ears. Kate noticed the exposed ear even then. Cal smiled. Kate smiled back and then looked down at the half-eaten melon.

"Oh shit," she said.

They both laughed.

"Are you planning to pay for that?" he asked. "Because my supervisor sent me over here to make sure you do."

"Yep," she said. She was staring at him.

They started talking, and before long Kate had invited him over for a drink. Just before Cal's shift ended, Kate brought the empty shell of the melon to the cash and paid for it. Cal asked if she'd like it in plastic or paper.

— • —

Cal turned over. Kate thought he was the most exquisite man or boy she had ever slept with. It wasn't a habit of Kate's to bring men home—especially boys—but something in her told her that this was the right thing to do. A voice in her head or in her heart. And she always listened to what her heart told her. She had Cal on the floor, against the wall, on the bed, on the dresser.... *Ohh...* Kate wrapped her arms around him and squeezed. He opened his eyes, one at a time. They were blue, they sparkled in the light; he was the real thing.

"Good morning," he said, his voice rough with sleep.

"Well, hello," Kate said.

He rubbed his eyes and looked around the room.

"I guess I wasn't dreaming after all."

"Nope," Kate said, and gave his nipple a little pinch.

She turned over and leaned on her elbows to look outside. The sun was shining, making shadows of the trees on the street. There was an early morning quality to the light, though it was nearly noon. Cal ran his fingers through Kate's hair. That's when she saw the other boy. He was small, maybe ten or eleven, and he stood looking in the window at them. He just stood there watching. He stared at Kate for a moment and then turned and walked away. It happened so quickly that Kate was not sure whether she had actually seen him or just imagined him.

"I think there's a peeping Tom out there," she said.

"Where?" Cal asked, turning.

Kate pointed to the window. She got up and wrapped the sheet around herself, leaving Cal naked on the bed. He turned on his side and watched her walk across the floor. The white sheet dragged behind her like the train of a wedding gown. Outside, the young boy who had been looking in the window was standing by the curb throwing stones out into the street. Kate watched him and tapped on the glass. He turned around and looked at her. She shrugged her shoulders at him and mouthed the words, *What do you want?*

The boy pointed with one of his little fingers to the porch and then pointed towards himself. Kate glanced at the porch. Cal's bike was locked to the railing. She called over her shoulder for Cal to come to the window.

He grabbed his jeans from the floor and pulled them on before approaching the window.

"Did you steal that kid's bike?" Kate asked, pointing to the boy by the curb.

Cal looked out the window.

"Oh, damn."

"What? You did steal his bike?"

"No, no. That's my little brother, Liam. I borrowed his bike. He must want it back."

Upon seeing Cal, Liam began pointing angrily towards his bike. Kate and Cal could both hear him through the window.

"I want my bike!"

Cal nodded and searched his pockets for the keys to the lock. He found them and dangled them for Liam to see. He turned to Kate.

"I'll be back in a minute."

"How the hell did he find you here?" she asked.

"Who knows. The kid's funny. He always finds me."

"Oh, so you do this all the time, do you?" Kate put her hands on her hips dramatically, nearly losing the sheet that was wrapped around her.

Cal smiled and walked out of the room with the keys jingling in his hand. As he passed through the doorway, Kate turned and looked out the window. Liam ran up the driveway to the porch as Cal emerged from the house. The neighbors would definitely have something to talk about now. Kate looked around at the other houses, but no one was out. She watched the two boys talk. The younger boy looked angry. He gestured wildly with his hands and pointed to the bike and then to the watch on his wrist. He leaned in close to Cal at one point and said something in his ear. Then both he and Cal turned to look at Kate standing there in the window. She didn't know what to do so she smiled and waved. They both turned away. Cal unlocked the bike and then stood there on the porch watching his brother ride off. He didn't come in until the boy was out of sight.

Kate dressed quickly and looked around for her earrings and the necklace with the cross on it. She found them on the floor next to the dresser where they had dropped the night before. She smiled as she did up the clasp of her necklace and then put on her earrings. Cal came in and got the rest of his clothes on.

"How did he find you?" Kate asked.

"He said he saw the bike on the porch when he was delivering the paper this morning." Cal paused. "Which is fine, except that he doesn't deliver the paper."

Kate laughed and gave Cal a kiss on the cheek.

"How about some breakfast?"

— • —

The kitchen was large and airy. There were windows on three sides; the curtains were wide open. Kate put some coffee on and leaned against the counter. The smell alone was enough to fully wake her. She watched Cal open the refrigerator and stand back. He bent down and reached in to shift some things around to get a better look. Empty handed, he closed the door and opened the cupboard next to the refrigerator. There were nearly a dozen cereal boxes on the shelves inside the cupboard. He pulled one out and opened it.

"Make yourself at home," Kate said.

"Whose house did you say this was?" he asked, stuffing cereal into his mouth.

"The couple who own the bookstore I work at. They're in Europe for a couple of months."

"Nice place," he said, looking around.

"Nicer than anyplace I've ever lived," Kate said.

"Where do you live?" Cal asked.

Kate got some fruit out of the refrigerator.

"In the summer, I live and work in Whitehorse. The rest of the time, I live wherever I end up. Preferably somewhere warm."

"What are you doing in Halifax?"

"I came to visit my family in the fall. I guess I never left. I'll probably head back up north in a couple of months."

"Sounds good," Cal said.

Kate watched him walk out of the room carrying the cereal box in his hands. His jeans were a couple sizes too big, and his t-shirt had a logo on it that Kate didn't recognize. He dressed like the skateboarders she saw riding around in front of the house; the same kids from down the street that were called in at night by their mothers.

"How old are these people?" Cal asked from the other room. "Have you seen the music they listen to? Neil Young. Joni Mitchell. Simon and Garfunkel? And Bach? Who listens to this stuff anymore?"

"I do," Kate said. "It's good music. You might like some of it."

She could hear him fiddling around with a CD and then pushing some buttons on the stereo.

"What did you find?" she asked.

"Some classical music that I can appreciate."

The music began too loudly for Kate to distinguish any melody. Cal turned it down slightly. It was Led Zeppelin. Kate hadn't listened to Led Zeppelin since high school. She immediately thought of those awkward high school dances and "Stairway to Heaven" and dancing with Todd Parks. His hands on her ass, holding her close and tight. She could remember the feeling of something that was not his belt buckle pushing into her belly. And Todd asking with a wink if she could feel his belt buckle poking her. Todd was tall. Todd was about the same age as her bag boy.

Cal came up behind where Kate stood cutting a grapefruit at the counter. He wrapped his arms around her and hugged her tightly.

"Careful," she warned, "I've got a knife in my hand."

"That's all right. I've handled worse."

His hands slid up under her shirt. He cupped her breasts and pulled Kate closer. He licked her neck.

"Again," he whispered into her ear.

Kate put the knife down and turned around to face Cal.

"Are you for real?"

Cal smiled and kissed her on the mouth.

"I like you a lot," he said. "I've never done this before."

Laughing, Kate pushed him away.

"Do you mean that before last night you were a…a virgin?" she asked. "Does that mean I have to marry you?"

"No, that's not what I mean. I…." Cal was trying to be serious. "I just…I really like you. You're not like other—"

"Don't say it. Please don't say it. You've only just met me."

Kate put her hand over Cal's mouth. She knew what he was going to say—and she didn't want to hear it. It reminded her too much of those high school days, and the things boys say.

Cal moved her hand away from his mouth.

"But—"

Kate made a gesture as if to brush it away.

"Never mind," she said. "Just kiss me."

They kissed and Cal pulled Kate down to the floor where they made love again. Kate could smell the coffee brewing and the grapefruit juice on her fingers. And the smell of the boy—sweat and yesterday's cologne. The music was loud and made Kate think of so many things at once, of the past and of the future. And for a moment, it seemed as if everything was as it should be.

— • —

The next month passed much like that first day. Cal spent most nights at the house with Kate, sleeping next to her between the cool sheets and eating breakfast with her before work. All month she felt resplendent, alive. Her face seemed to glow; it was brilliant. Her days were spent working and humming Led Zeppelin tunes. And after work, she would walk over to Sobey's to see her bag boy and pick up a few groceries. She made late suppers for them to eat when Cal got off work. And sometimes they'd eat out in the yard. They even made love in the grass once, after the neighbors had all gone to bed. Afterwards, they sat on the kitchen floor by the light of the refrigerator and threw grapes into each other's mouths from across the room. They talked about plans and about dreams. Cal wanted to go back to school to become a high school teacher. Kate wanted to settle down some day and have a small farm and sell fruit and vegetables and eggs in the country.

She was not sure where any of it was going. She still intended to leave in the spring, and as much fun as she was having with Cal, she couldn't really imagine a long-term relationship with someone so young, so different. She'd get bored, the way she always did. And then she'd find herself on her way out of town. Might as well just leave and avoid the rest, the possible heartache, the scene that would surely follow.

By the end of April, she told Cal she was going to return to Whitehorse; she told him she *had* to return. Though she had mentioned it to him when they first met, he acted as if it was the first time he was hearing these plans of hers. He ignored her at first, and Kate thought he would try to convince her to either stay or bring him along. She wasn't willing to do either; she had made up her mind.

She got the paper one morning and sat looking at ads for flight specials while Cal did push-ups on the kitchen floor. His shirt was on the floor beside him, next to Kate's shoes. She'd look over at him every now and then, and smile.

"You're lovely," she said.

"Is that good?" Cal asked from the floor.

He was upset this particular morning because they'd had a talk the night before, and Kate had suggested—without coming out and saying it—that she didn't want him tagging along with her up north.

"You knew all along that I was planning to leave in the spring. And now it's almost summer. I can't stay here. My parents live here. And besides, I have a job to get back to."

"You hardly ever see your parents. And what about me? What about us?"

Cal looked up at her.

"Us," she said.

"Yeah. If you stay we could maybe look for a small place together...."

"Move in together?"

"Yeah. We practically live together now. You said so yourself."

She had considered the possibility—briefly, when it was all still fresh—of staying, moving in with Cal. She wanted to be in love, and to stay in love. She wanted it more than anything. But it hardly ever happened. And she had lost faith in the possibility, had resigned herself to never being satisfied. It seemed she was always leaving someone behind, and always would be: she got used to it after a while, in the way some people get used to small pets dying.

"I said it was like we were *playing* house," Kate said after a minute. "And that's different."

Cal continued doing push-ups.

"Nothing lasts forever," Kate said. She circled a couple of ads. "They expect me to return. I have a job."

"Whatever." Cal counted under his breath. "Forty-nine. Fifty."

He stood up and pulled his shirt over his head. Kate watched him drink straight from the carton of orange juice that was on the table. A thin orange stream ran down his chin. He wiped it away with the back of his hand and turned to go. Kate looked back down at the paper.

"Well, good-bye," he said.

"Don't get mad, Cal. You knew I was leaving."

"I thought you'd change your mind," he said, and then turned and walked out of the room.

— • —

Kate's period was three weeks late. She thought nothing of it at first. She made up a rhyme that sounded like a page out of a children's book.

"Late Kate. Kate is late. Look at Kate be late."

But Cal didn't laugh. He picked up a book and stared blankly at its pages. He had come to visit Kate at the bookstore. She was straightening out some shelves, dusting and sneezing. The owners of the store, and of the house, would be back in just two weeks, and Kate would be leaving town shortly thereafter. They had decided to make the best of their time together, she and Cal.

"Don't worry," she said. "I'm just late. No sense getting worried about it right now."

Cal still said nothing.

"What are you thinking?" Kate asked. "What's going through your mind right now?"

She walked over to the counter and sat down.

"Do you think that you are…pregnant? Do you feel pregnant?"

He looked terrified. His eyes were big and wild; his voice was shaky, uneven. And Kate saw suddenly how young he really was, and how scared he was. She could imagine him and his brother, Liam, playing video games at home or basketball in the park. And he seemed not like the man she was sleeping with but like the child that looked in the window that morning, so young.

"No. I don't think so," she said.

A customer came into the store and Cal said a quick good-bye and left.

— • —

Late indeed, thought Kate. It seemed unbelievable. It seemed, to Kate, just preposterous. It was so unlikely. How could it be? she wondered. They were so careful; they were usually careful, anyway. Kate tried to recall every time they made love. She wasn't on the pill because she didn't like the idea of taking pills. And so it was condoms, which weren't foolproof.

A few days later, when Kate was still late, she went out and bought a pregnancy test without telling Cal. She downplayed her real concerns to him; let on that it was no big deal, nothing to worry about. But she did *feel* different, her body felt different. She did the test one night when Cal was at work. She sat on the toilet and held the little stick under the stream of urine. Then she waited.

The test was positive. The box claimed the test was accurate 99% of the time.

Sitting there on the toilet, Kate tried to envision what a new baby would look like: small and round and pink, she imagined, like a plucked turkey, only cute. Maybe, she thought, this will turn things around, straighten things out. Maybe this was the thing she had been expecting, not knowing what it was. This was the crossroads.

She got changed and walked over to Sobey's to talk to Cal. It was getting warmer everyday; the coming of summer was suggested in the air, in the smell of trees and grass and mud. It was close to dusk, the sunlight shimmered through the branches above her as she walked. She had no plan, wasn't sure how she'd bring it up or what she'd say. She felt as though she was walking in slow motion. The air around her was still, nothing seemed to move at all.

Cal was standing outside eating potato chips and talking to one of his co-workers, a young woman Kate had seen working at the check-out. When Kate saw Cal from across the parking lot, she began to cry uncontrollably. She didn't want to tell him; she didn't want to deal with anything. She thought about turning around and walking back home, packing up and leaving without a word. But it wouldn't be that simple. Not anymore. Things had changed suddenly. Moments ago, she was another person, living another life. And now she was someone else altogether.

Cal noticed Kate across the parking lot. He said something to his co-worker and she went back inside. Kate wiped at the tears and walked over.

"Are you all right?" he asked

Kate tried to think of some way to say it, to tell him in such a way as to make it sound like good news.

"I'm pregnant," was all she said.

Cal's eyes widened. He looked around to see if anyone was close enough to have heard.

"Are you sure?" he whispered.

"Yes," Kate said.

"Did you.... How do you know?" He was thunderstruck.

"I just did a test."

They stood side by side, silent. Kate looked at him, said nothing. Cal tried to speak but remained quiet. Someone called his name.

"I have to get back in. We'll talk later. Okay?"

Kate nodded, and Cal turned and walked away without saying good-bye. She stood there and watched people walk past. She wished she were any one of them.

Somehow she managed to walk back to the house where she sat out in the yard for a while. The sky was clear. Away from the lights, she could see thousands of stars, like pin pricks letting in light from somewhere beyond all that darkness. Sitting there in the grass where she and Cal had made love weeks before, she began to cry again. It was impossible. There was just no way. She wasn't ready for this. The phone rang but Kate ignored it. *Nothing is easy.* No decision, no plan, nothing. How did other people do it? she wondered. How did they decide to have kids? Or to not have kids? Kate held her head in her hands, not crying anymore, not feeling anything for a while. It seemed unreal.

The phone rang again an hour later. This time Kate ran inside and answered. It was Cal. He said he wouldn't make it over because he had to work late. He'd come over in the morning and they could talk then. Kate hung up and walked into the bathroom. She splashed cold water on her face. And as she dried off, she thought, *Things like this happen all the time. Things fall from the sky and hit you on the head—Bang. And they knock you down for a while but then you get back up and move on. Don't you? You do, don't you? Please say you do....* She rubbed her flat stomach. She couldn't believe there was something—someone in there. She couldn't believe the things she was thinking.

— • —

It was dark and night had covered everything in its shade. If there were any answers, any voices telling her what she should do, Kate couldn't hear them. Night makes everything seem so much more difficult, so impossible. Nothing seems easy at night. Being alone, making a decision, just figuring things out: it all becomes frustratingly, sadly impossible. Like falling in a well and then trying to climb up the smooth, wet walls. Kate sat on the floor, afraid to move, and waited for morning to come, waited for her heart to start speaking to her. But it took a long, long time.

— • —

In the morning, Kate's neck was sore. She had fallen asleep leaning against the wall in the bathroom. The only thing that had changed was that it was light outside. Morning had finally arrived, but that light had not erased the night before. Everything else was the same. Kate felt her stomach again. Nothing. She got up to make some coffee. She hesitated, remembering what she had read once about caffeine during pregnancy, but then she went ahead and made it anyway.

At one point during the morning, Kate decided she could not keep the baby, could not *have* the baby. It happened when she was filling a glass with water. It just struck her: "I can't do this." She spoke the words aloud, slowly, measured. She had thought she could. She had woken up in the night, her neck twisted, her head resting on her shoulder, and she thought: *Yes, this is what I need to settle down: a baby will keep me true.* And then she fell back asleep. But after many confusing dreams, she realized that it is a heavy weight to place on such small shoulders. And like falling down stairs, a thousand things tumbled through her mind at once until she had to hit her head against the wall to slow it down.

A little later in the day she heard a knock at the door. It was raining heavily. Kate had the windows closed and the curtains drawn.

She opened the door. Cal's brother, Liam, was standing outside on the porch, soaking wet. He had his bike with him.

She invited him in, but he shook his head.

"I have a letter for you," he said.

"I see you've gone from being a repo-man to a mail-man." She smiled weakly.

He looked up blankly and then dug into his pocket for the letter. The envelope was wet. Her name was printed in blue ink on the front. The ink was smudged.

"What's this?" Kate asked, looking up and down the street.

"A letter from Cal."

"He couldn't deliver it himself?"

Liam shrugged his shoulders and handed her the letter.

"Thanks," she said.

"Welcome."

Liam turned and walked his bike down the driveway. He had a long, dark strip on his back from water coming off the back wheel of his bike. He looked over his shoulder at Kate and then got on his bike and rolled away.

She opened the envelope there on the porch. She was already crying before she finished unfolding it.

Dear Kate, it began, *I'm sorry I didn't come over last night but I need some time to think about this. When you told me the news yesterday, I nearly passed out. I couldn't sleep all night. I can't imagine being a father. I'm not ready for that, not yet. And with you leaving. It's as if this thing is some kind of test. I know I'm probably failing right now but I don't know what else to do. I'll call you. Love, Cal*

She couldn't move. She didn't try. *So that was it. That was it.*

— • —

Kate called Cal later that day, but his mother said he wasn't home. She wanted to tell his mother then, I'm pregnant with your son's baby. But she said nothing, hung up. Later that night she heard a knock at the door and expected to see Liam on the porch again but this time it was Cal.

"Hi," he said.

He came in out of the rain.

"What are you going to do?" he asked.

"What am *I* going to do?"

"What are *we* going to do?"

"I take it you don't want to have this baby with me?"

"It's not that.... I'm just not ready, Kate. Jesus, I'm eighteen. And a few days ago, you were planning to leave town, and leave me."

"Then I guess I'll have an abortion."

She spoke matter-of-factly. She wanted him to say no, but he only looked at her and then at something on the wall. Kate walked out of the hall and sat down in the living room.

"Is that what you want?" Cal asked, following her.

"What do you want, Cal? What do you want to do?" Her voice rose above her normal speaking voice.

"I don't know. I'm not ready for this," he said again.

"I guess you should have thought of that before—" But she stopped, looked out the window. It was cloudy; the light was hazy and gray. "What if I went ahead and had the baby. You wouldn't have to do anything. You'd be like a sperm donour."

But that's not really what she wanted.

Cal paced around the room. He turned on the TV and changed the channel a few times before turning it off again. When he placed the remote control back on the coffee table, he knocked a glass onto the floor. It shattered on the ground at his feet.

"Fuck," he said.

He threw the remote control across the room. Kate watched him but made no move to get up.

"Can we talk about this without smashing things on the floor and throwing things across the room?"

Cal picked up the broken glass and carried it to the kitchen.

"I can't do this alone. You're acting like it's my fault this happened," Kate said.

Cal walked back into the living room.

"I'm sorry. I don't know what to do."

"Will you come with me to the clinic?"

He nodded his head and sat down across from her.

— • —

A few days passed before Kate made the call. She thought she'd have to get some tests done, to make sure. But the woman at the clinic told her to just come in. The appointment was in less than a week.

"Won't it be too late then?" Kate asked.

"No, dear," said the woman on the other end of the line. "No, it won't be too late."

Kate cringed when the woman called her dear. It reminded her of her mother.

At work, Kate tried her best to pretend everything was fine. And with Cal, she told him again and again that this was what she wanted. He came around during the week, but they no longer slept together. Kate said it was for the best.

"As soon as this is over," she told him, "I'm flying to Whitehorse. I have my ticket and everything."

Cal said nothing. And she knew it was really over. And even though that was what she wanted all along, it now seemed mixed up in her mind nothing seemed right.

— • —

Cal made arrangements to borrow his mother's car the day of the appointment. When he picked Kate up at the house, Liam was sitting in the passenger seat. Kate stood at the curb without getting in and looked at Cal.

"It was the only way I could get the car," he said. "I couldn't tell her where I was going."

He told Liam to get in the back seat. But Kate said it was okay, that she'd sit back there. They drove in silence to the clinic. Liam put the radio on at one point, but Cal reached over and turned it off. Kate changed her mind a hundred times along the way but always returned to her decision to go through with the abortion. She knew a few women who had abortions but they rarely talked about it, and most of them had had them when they were much younger than Kate. Her women friends were now at an age where they were either already parents or trying to get pregnant. Kate felt very alone.

Cal parked the car in a lot down the street from the clinic. Liam pulled some comic books out of his backpack and stayed in the car. Kate didn't know if he knew where she was going; and she didn't want to ask.

"See you," he said, when Kate walked past his open window.

She had expected protesters with Molotov cocktails, placards declaring that she personally was a cold-blooded killer. She had rehearsed in her mind what she would do. She wouldn't scurry past like they always did on TV, with her head down and buried somewhere in her coat protecting herself from who knows what. She would walk in brazenly, a serious expression on her face, her gaze fixed and hard as steel. Maybe she'd tell them off. But there was no one there, no one was waiting outside to pelt her with rotten tomatoes like some cheap actor on a stage. It was early, the streets were just starting to fill up with people in business suits. They walked by, oblivious.

She and Cal stood outside the door. Kate took a deep breath. And then slowly, Cal opened the door and they walked up the stairs one at a time. It was eerily quiet. At the top of the stairs was another door. They opened it and walked in. A woman sat at a desk behind a bullet-proof window. She smiled at Kate and spoke into a microphone.

"Do you have an appointment?"

Kate looked up at the speaker.

"Yes...I do."

"Do you have your health card?"

Kate took it out of her wallet and slipped it through a small opening in the window. The woman looked at it and then up at Kate.

"Will your friend be coming in with you?"

"Yes."

"I'll get the door for you both."

The door to Kate's right clicked. And the woman from behind the window was waiting for them when they opened the door and walked in.

"My name's Helen." She held out her hand. "This way, please."

They walked down a hallway and into a room. Cal followed behind. There were a few other people waiting in the room. Mostly women. Some looked up nervously at Kate and Cal. A young woman in sweatpants and a tight T-shirt looked up with a bored expression on her face. She sat reading a magazine, and every once in a while she would look at her nails and pick at her cuticles. There was just one other man in the room. He, too, had a magazine on his lap, but it remained unopened. He appeared nervous or embarrassed to be sitting in there with all those women. His baseball cap was pulled down over his eyes, and he sat there looking down at his shoes. Occasionally, he'd look around the room at the other people sitting there, but he avoided eye contact.

Helen handed Kate a sheet of paper and a pen.

"Fill this out as much as you can," she said. "Your name will be called shortly."

Kate stared at the medical history form. The words meant nothing to her. She filled it out absently. And before long her name was called. Cal touched her arm.

"Good luck," he said.

Kate didn't say anything. A woman came and lead her to another room.

"We're just going to check your vitals and do a few tests."

"Okay," Kate said.

She sat on a bed and took off her shirt. The woman was busy preparing the things she would need. Kate sat quietly and waited. She tried to keep her eyes closed, but she couldn't. The woman explained the procedure to Kate and asked if she had any fears or worries. Kate laughed nervously.

"I'm just not ready," she said.

"Not ready to have the abortion?"

"Yes. No. I mean, I'm not ready to…to be a mother."

The woman stopped what she was doing and looked at Kate earnestly. Her eyes were squinting, and a few wrinkles creased the bridge of her nose. She nodded her head slowly.

"No. It is a lot of work. And it is forever. Sometimes you just have to do what you think is right for you at that particular time. Is this right for you now, Kate?"

Kate nodded her head.

The woman asked if Kate wanted to talk any more about it or about anything at all. But Kate said no. She didn't feel like talking. She didn't feel like doing anything. She just wanted to sit under a tree and forget about it all. But she was inside—and outside was so very far away.

In the room where they performed the abortion, Kate lay on another bed and stared up at the ceiling. The room was brightly lit. Kate squinted and looked around once for an emergency exit, but she didn't see one and so she looked back up at the ceiling. There was a nurse in the room with her busy preparing things in the corner. Another woman walked in and began speaking to Kate. Kate nodded her head, barely listening.

The woman began prodding Kate's belly.

"...to feel the size and position of the uterus," she explained.

Kate took a deep breath and was resigned—in that brief moment when she could feel the air filling her lungs—to go through with it.

"Okay," she said to no one in particular. "I'm okay."

She felt something cold and metallic enter her vagina. She tried to think of something pleasant. But, eyes opened or closed, she could only see a blur of light. She felt small pains like contractions in her uterus. She tried to breathe deeply, regularly. She waited it out.

— • —

And then it was over. They put Kate in a small room to rest. The light was softer; she almost fell asleep. There was a window in the room, covered with aluminum blinds. She could see between the cracks of the blinds to the city outside and across the city to the hills and the forest and away—north. In a few days, she would be on a plane heading out of town. And this would all be over. Her mind was empty for a moment, and she could just look out the window and not think of anything. Someone came in to see how she was doing and the hills disappeared. And it all came back to her. She was on her feet, being escorted from the room by a woman she had never seen before.

Cal rose when she entered the waiting room. He walked over to Kate and put his arm around her.

"I'll go get the car and pick you up out front."

Before she could reply, say that all she really wanted was to get outside herself, he was gone and someone else was speaking to her, making an appointment she wouldn't keep. She felt sick and heavy walking down the stairs afterwards—not light, as she had hoped she would. She just wanted out. She held tightly to the railing—her head reeled, the light came and went, darkness sometimes closed in on her. And then the tears came—before she even reached the door at the bottom of the stairs that would lead her outside into the goddamn beautiful sun, the tears came. Her eyes flooded; her sight became obscured like a camera lens covered with Vaseline. *Jesus Christ.* She wiped angrily at the tears in her eyes with her sleeve. It smelled medicinal and made her feel even more nauseous. *Shitshitshit.* The tears kept coming like blood from a wound that would not be staunched. She tried to look through the window at the bottom of the stairs; she tried to see the car that should be waiting for her there—but her eyes continued to flood with tears. She could see only a blur of ugly light, and nothing else.

THE NATURE OF MAPS

I can't believe you just did that!" Ingrid said, pushing past Marty. He rolled his eyes at her, but she wasn't looking; she was already outside with the door closing behind her. They had spent the last three and a half hours in a movie theatre watching *Seven Samurai* and it was now quite late. Marty was tired and not at all up to trying to smooth things over with Ingrid. He wanted to be home in bed, or even alone on the couch with the TV playing quietly, the blue flickering light dancing on the walls—but it was never that simple. He slipped through the door and caught up with her outside.

There were a few people standing in front of the theatre zipping up their coats and pulling their hats down over their ears. It was late February and still rather cold. Marty took Ingrid's hand and tried to lead her past two men pretending to draw swords, but she pulled free and walked on ahead. He stopped and waited for her to turn, to notice he wasn't following, but she walked all the way to the corner where she stood waiting for the light to change. The two men with pretend swords danced around on the sidewalk beside Marty. He overheard one of the men say to the other, "If this sword were real, I'd have killed you."

At the corner, Marty took hold of Ingrid's hand again and gently played his index finger on her palm. Her hand was cold and limp. She said nothing. Smiling cautiously, he twisted his neck to look into her eyes. She remained staring straight ahead, watching the traffic light across the street. When the light changed, she stepped into the street so abruptly she nearly dragged Marty along because he refused to let go of her hand.

"I was being polite," he said, after they had crossed the street. She still said nothing.

"What was I supposed to do? Tell her, 'No thanks, I already have a phone number?'" He was trying to be funny. "Come on, Ing."

Ingrid didn't laugh; she didn't even smile. Marty waited for her to say something, anything.

"Polite!" she said after another block. But that was all she said.

"Can I really help it if some woman I hardly know gives me her phone number?" Marty asked.

"It's not just that, Marty." She kept walking. "You stood there talking to her while I waited five feet away. For all I know, you didn't even tell her you were there with someone else."

Ingrid slipped her hand out of his and pushed it deep into her pocket. Her jaw was tense, her lips were pursed. Marty stopped walking.

"You were speaking to someone." He spoke slowly and raised his hands a little and tilted his head in a gesture that said, what gives?—which was an expression he often used.

"I was not," said Ingrid, stopping a few feet ahead of him. "Some guy asked me for the time and I gave it to him."

"You could have walked over and introduced yourself," Marty said.

He watched a bus pass by on the other side of the street. It turned the corner at the lights and disappeared. It was too late and too cold for this, he decided.

"That's not the point," Ingrid said. "I'm just saying it was a little odd to watch some woman hit on you and then to watch you just stand there, not letting on at all that you were with me, your girlfriend—remember? And then you take the number from her. What would you do if I did that to you?"

"I'd walk over and put my arm around you."

"You would not."

"Ingrid, it's not a big deal—"

"You didn't even bother to introduce me. Not even as a *friend*—which you've done in the past."

Marty reached into his pocket and pulled out the slip of paper with the woman's phone number on it.

"Here," he said, thrusting the paper at Ingrid. "Tear it up and throw it away. I'm not going to call her. I accepted it to be polite."

Ingrid folded her arms on her chest.

"I'm not doing your dirty work."

"Dirty work? What are you talking about?" He was exasperated.

"You throw it out," she said.

"Fine."

"Fine."

Ingrid walked away and Marty stared at the paper. The woman's name was printed in thin, looping lines. Lucy, it said. And then below that, the number. He looked for a garbage can but there wasn't one in sight. He didn't want to just drop her number on the ground; it required more ceremony than that. And besides, he wanted Ingrid to see him do it, so he could prove to her how foolish she was being about it all. He really wasn't interested in the woman; she was just someone he remembered from a while ago, someone from his past. He slipped the paper back into his pocket and ran to catch up with Ingrid.

"I'm sorry," he said.

"It's okay."

They walked in silence for a couple of blocks. A cold wind coming off the side of a high-rise whipped around them. Marty put his arm around Ingrid's shoulder and held her tightly. Her nose and cheeks were cold and red. She wore a toque, but no gloves, and only a thin ski jacket. It had been a crisp day though the sun had shone brightly making it seem milder than it really was. Marty looked over his shoulder occasionally—the street was mostly deserted now. A taxi drove by. And then another. Ingrid was shivering.

"Do you want to get a cab?" Marty asked, looking up and down the street for another taxi.

"No. I'll be fine."

"We could have a warm bath when we get home," he suggested.

"Sure."

Ingrid looked at him and smiled. He pulled her in close, and she nuzzled into his shoulder. She started talking about the movie, and Marty was grateful because it meant that she was perhaps over the *other* thing, at least for the time being. She had seen the movie once before and had memorized some of the lines. Marty fell asleep and missed almost an hour. He rubbed his eyes tiredly when the lights came on in the theatre and said that falling asleep hadn't really affected his understanding of the plot since he only missed a third of the movie. He said that nothing much happened anyway. And then he got up to go. To spite him, Ingrid stayed in her seat until the last credits rolled by in Japanese and English. Marty waited by the doors. That was when the woman recognized him and ran over. And then gave him her phone number. Ingrid was on her way over to where Marty stood talking to the woman, but a man stopped her and asked for the time. When she looked back at the two of them, the woman was handing Marty her number and saying goodbye.

"If you think nothing happened in that movie, then you clearly missed the point," Ingrid was saying. "There's so much going on. It's an investigation into the past and its meaning in modern society. It's about social justice and the promise of community. And then there's Mifune. How could you fall asleep on a man like that? With that voice? He's really something else. You know, Kurosawa said of him that...."

But Marty wasn't listening. Ingrid often went on like this, as though she were reading straight from a text book, which she could have been for all he knew. Marty had no interest in films or directors or actors; he tended to let his mind wander when Ingrid talked about these things. He'd nod his head, or try to look interested, as if he were considering her remarks and waiting to make a comment of his own. Ingrid had studied film in Montreal before she and Marty met, and now she was a member of the local film co-op. Nearly all of her spare time was devoted to working on a film or video with other members of the co-op. Every month there seemed to be a shoot somewhere in town. They once had a small film crew shooting in their apartment, and Marty was used as an extra: an extra in his own home. That was the last time he agreed to do that.

What did interest Marty were maps. Maps were full of mystery and potential; they attempted to make sense of the world around, simplifying it, reducing it to lines and colours and the names of places. He pinned up maps on the walls at home the way most people pin up artwork and posters. On the wall by the front door of their apartment was a large framed map of the world. It was the first thing one saw upon entering. A flattened representation of the earth, was how Marty referred to it. He could spend hours looking at it, tracing lines north and south, east and west, looking for countries and cities he'd like to visit. Sometimes he'd close his eyes and randomly place his finger on the map. Then, opening his eyes, he'd read the name of the place he'd pointed to and go find it in one of his old atlases. He knew the capital of almost every country; it had become a party trick: pick a country, any country. He often complained to Ingrid about not pursuing his love of maps. And he regretted not finding employment in his field, geography. He worked in the reference department of the public library.

Marty looked at his watch. It was half-past midnight. The air was cold, the wind stinging. He looked down at the sidewalk to keep his face out of the wind. The snow on the sidewalk and by the side of the road was dirty and gray, no longer resembling snow. It had been a long, cold winter, and despite occasional respite, spring still seemed far, far away. He tried to remember the feeling of warm sun on his skin, of a warm breeze through his hair. Ingrid was asking him a question.

"Who is she anyway?"

Marty looked at her for a moment, as if he was trying to remember who she, Ingrid, was and not the woman from the movie theatre.

"Oh, some girl I took a class with when I was in university. We used to talk sometimes."

"And she remembered you?" Ingrid asked.

"I guess so. It wasn't that long ago."

He answered as if it didn't matter one way or the other who the woman was or why she remembered him and gave him her phone number. He wanted Ingrid to forget about it; he didn't want it to lead to where he knew it would eventually lead. He had made some mistakes in the past, it was true, but surely one could forget, forgive. It had been a long time.

"What does she do now?" Ingrid asked.

"She teaches geography and english at some high school."

"She must have liked you then."

Marty looked at her.

"Why do you say that?"

"Because she remembered you. And gave you her number. Did you two ever...."

"No." He sighed and then stopped walking. "I barely know her. We went out for drinks after an exam once. I'm sorry I took the number. And I'm sorry I didn't introduce you. I made a mistake. Now, can we drop it?"

Ingrid took his hand and continued walking.

"Okay."

"I'm cold and tired and I want to get home."

He walked a little faster, stepping out into the street against the light. Ingrid jogged along side him to the other side. At Cobourg Street, they turned north and then cut across MacDonald Park. The park was dotted with trees, but mostly it was bare and gray under the clouded and dark sky. They walked diagonally across, towards the North side. To their right was a small hill covered with trampled snow and ice and topped with a stone gazebo. During the day, children slid down the hill, filling the park with shouts and screams. But there was no one in sight as the two of them walked along the path.

"There was a cemetery here years ago," Marty said, slowing down a little to look around.

"Really?"

"Yes. Someone came into the library a while ago looking for an old map of the park. She said she was writing about it. Anyway, they moved the whole cemetery to another location in 1872." He pointed to the ground beneath their feet. "This was the Roman Catholic section right here."

Ingrid shuddered and looked around the park. The moon had broken through some clouds overhead and cast a cool light over them, but it soon disappeared as more clouds moved in. At the end of the path was a stairway leading down to the street. On either side of the stairs were trees, bare and thin, which kept that corner of the park in shadows. As they approached the staircase, a man stepped out from behind a gathering of trees and stood in the path before them. He was tall and bulky in an oversized black jacket. His hands were in his pockets.

"Got the time?" the man asked.

Ingrid tightened her grip on Marty's arm. Marty pulled up his sleeve to look at his watch.

"While you're at it," the man said, "give me your wallets."

Marty laughed. He thought the man had to be joking; he had never been mugged before. Ingrid gasped, and when Marty looked up at the man, he saw that he was holding a knife.

"What gives?" Marty asked.

"This," said the mugger, indicating the knife. "The wallet. The watch. And anything else you've got. You too." He pointed the knife at Ingrid.

"Don't hurt us," Marty said weakly.

The mugger didn't say anything.

Ingrid quickly took off her watch and handed it to the mugger along with her wallet. Marty did the same.

"Any jewelry?" the mugger asked.

Ingrid unclasped the necklace Marty had given her for their second anniversary and reluctantly handed it to the mugger. Marty slipped off his class ring and handed that over. The mugger looked at Ingrid's hand. She wore a large diamond ring that had once belonged to her grandmother.

"That one, too," he said, pointing to the ring with his knife.

"Please let me keep it. It's a fake. It belonged to my grandmother."

Marty looked from Ingrid to the mugger.

"Let her keep it," Marty pleaded.

"Is your grandmother dead?" the mugger asked.

"Yes."

"Then she won't mind, will she?"

Ingrid struggled to get the ring off her finger.

"It's stuck," she said, looking up at the mugger.

"Then I'll have to cut it off."

He didn't laugh or smile, but only looked at Ingrid and waited. After pulling at the ring for another few seconds, she got it off and handed it to him. Marty put his arm around her and held her close. There were tears in her eyes.

"There," Marty said. "We've given you everything we have."

The mugger looked at them for a moment before speaking. His lips slowly curled into a smile.

"No, not everything," he said. "Gimme your jackets."

"You're kidding, right?" Marty asked.

"No." He was still smiling.

"Come on, man. We'll freeze," Marty said.

"That's not my problem."

Ingrid began to unzip her jacket but Marty stopped her.

"You got what you wanted," Marty said. "Just let us go. Don't do this."

"Shut the fuck up and give me your jackets."

They did as they were told. The mugger stuffed their jackets under his arm and took a quick look around the park. It was empty throughout. He looked back at Marty and Ingrid.

"Well," said Marty. Ingrid squeezed his arm. "Can we please go? Please."

The mugger held the knife out towards them. The blade looked dull in the pale light. Marty imagined kicking it out of his hand, wrestling him to the ground. But he only stood there, waiting for it to be over. Finally, the mugger turned to go.

"Asshole," Marty said under his breath.

Ingrid gave him a scared look and tugged at his arm. The mugger slowly turned around to face them.

"What'd you say?"

They were both silent.

"What did you say?" the mugger asked again.

"Nothing," said Marty.

The mugger took a step forward.

"Nothing, eh? Tough guy."

He looked at Marty and dropped the jackets on the ground.

"Tell me what you said."

"Please just let us go," Ingrid begged. "We're sorry. He didn't mean anything by it."

He ignored Ingrid and continued walking towards Marty.

"Tell me what you said." He pushed Marty on the shoulder. "Just tell me what you said and I'll let you go."

He pushed him again.

"Asshole," whispered Marty. "I said asshole."

The mugger punched him right in the face. Marty saw it coming but there was nothing he could do; it happened so fast. He thought he heard the bones cracking in his nose as the mugger's fist made contact. But it was only the sound of snow crunching under the mugger's feet. Marty fell back, holding his face in his hands. And Ingrid screamed. The mugger grabbed their jackets and ran down the snow covered steps and away.

Ingrid knelt down next to Marty and put her arm around him.

"Are you all right?" she asked.

Marty sat in the snow, still holding his face in his hands. He looked at Ingrid.

"A good samurai will parry the blow," he said. It was the only thing he remembered from the movie.

There was blood dripping from his nose, over his lips and down to his chin. Drops of blood fell and speckled the snow like small black holes before him. He reached into his pocket and pulled out a handkerchief. Ingrid took it from him and began dabbing at the blood.

"I've never been punched in the face before," Marty said. "It hurts like hell. I think he broke my nose."

"Why did you have to say that to him?" she asked.

"At least he didn't use the knife."

"Let's go," Ingrid said. "Let's go home."

Marty grabbed a fistful of snow and held it to his nose. He let Ingrid help him to his feet, and then they walked, holding one another, down the steps and out onto the street. They looked up and down the street, but there was no sign of the mugger anywhere. A block from the park, they passed a man walking his dog. He looked at them curiously but said nothing. They continued past, down a small hill, and towards the St. Patrick Street Bridge. A few cars drove by trailing thick exhaust in the cold night air. At the eastern end of the bridge, they could see the streetlights, now yellow, now red. And the cars stopped there, waiting. And the headlights of other cars coming towards them. To their right, and down, the river was still mostly frozen. Though there was a large opening in the ice, revealing the water that continued to flow beneath it towards the falls. The streetlights reflected darkly in the water, rippling with the current.

"I'm sorry about what happened earlier," Marty said. He still held the snow to his nose; he shivered, and his teeth chattered. "I should have introduced you. As my girlfriend. I'm sorry."

"It's okay," Ingrid said. "I guess I still get a little insecure sometimes, though. It just takes a while," she was quiet for a moment before finishing, "to rebuild trust."

Ingrid looked over at him and smiled without opening her mouth. As soon as she turned away, the smile left her face. Marty tossed the bloody snowball into the street. He watched it break apart and scatter.

"I know," he said. And then added, "That was a long time ago."

He pulled the piece of paper with the number on it out of his pocket and held it up over his head. His lips parted to speak, but instead he remained silent and just watched the paper in his hand. After a moment he loosened his fingers, and the paper was picked up by the wind. It rose above their heads like a small white bird and fluttered over the railing, high above the ice and water. And then it began a slow gentle fall to the ice where it was lost momentarily in the shadowed whiteness there. Marty took Ingrid's hand in his and peered over the railing. He searched the ice, hoping for some kind of sign that would tell him what to say to make everything better— like finding a map when you're lost. But all he saw was the paper skimming across the ice into the dark open water. For a moment it floated there, a white scrap on the imposing black surface, rising and falling with the current before finally being pulled down into the blackness of the river, under the ice and away.

IT'S ABOUT US

*P*aula was waiting at the corner for her daughter's school bus to arrive when Alex appeared out of nowhere wearing fake glasses with a fake nose and mustache attached. It was Halloween. Paula recognized him immediately.

"Where did you come from?" she asked. She looked around for a car, one she could imagine Alex driving—an old beat up Volkswagen or Volvo—as long as it wasn't American.

"From the clouds," Alex replied, smiling and pointing to the clear blue October sky.

He hadn't changed a bit. He was still skinny and his thin brown hair was no longer, no shorter than the last time she saw him—which was nearly a year ago. He was wearing jeans and a buttoned-up denim jacket. And when he smiled, she noticed his teeth needed cleaning. But he was still handsome. Behind the goofy smile and the disguise, the bad teeth and all that denim, he was still handsome.

"You look great," he said.

"What are you doing here?" Paula asked.

"I came to see you and Cora. I missed you both." He spread his arms wide, tilted his head a little to the right. "Hey, don't I get a hug?" he asked.

Paula reached over without moving her feet from where she stood. She put one arm around Alex's neck and gave the slightest squeeze before letting go.

"And a kiss?" he asked.

"No kiss."

"So." He stood with his hands deep in his pockets, watching her. "What's new? Carl still in the picture?"

"Yes, Carl's still in the picture. He's living with us now. He's asked me to marry him." She hesitated, watching Alex for a reaction. "And he wants to legally adopt Cora."

Alex looked down at her bare ring finger and then back up to her face.

"And what'd you tell him?"

"I said, we'd wait and see."

"I guess you were just waiting to talk to me about it, then."

"No. As a matter of fact, it didn't even cross my mind to talk to you about it, Alex."

"Are you still mad?"

"If I was still mad that would prove I still cared. Which I don't. I knew we were never in it for the long haul. I knew what to expect—or what not to expect from you." She paused. "Where've you been this time?"

"Here and there. Mostly there. I had a job out west for a while."

"It didn't occur to you to call?"

"I wrote."

"Yeah. A postcard that said, *Having a wonderful time. Wish you were here.* Original."

Alex smiled and kicked a small stone on the sidewalk. It rolled out into the street, nearly falling through a sewer grate. His hands were still deep in his pockets. He shrugged. They stood opposite one another for a moment, each silently waiting for the other to say something.

Before long, the school bus turned the corner. Paula could see Cora stand up and walk towards the front of the bus. The doors opened and the bus driver said hello to Paula. She nodded hello back. Alex was still wearing his disguise, and the bus driver watched him curiously. Even with the disguise, one could see the resemblance between Cora and Alex: the thin, pale lips set above a slightly pointed chin; and the dimpled cheeks when they smiled. Cora jumped down from the bottom step to the sidewalk. She was wearing a tiger costume, with tiger stripes painted on her face and a short tiger tail hanging limply behind her. She gave Paula a hug and looked up at Alex. The bus pulled away.

"Say hi to Uncle Alex, Cora." Paula looked at Alex. "Please take that thing off your face, Alex."

Alex took off his glasses and folded them up. He looked at Paula and mouthed the word "uncle?" But Paula just shrugged her shoulders.

"Hi," Cora said, holding on to her mother's leg.

"Hi, kid," Alex said. "Are you supposed to be Tigger?"

Cora's face brightened.

"Yeah!"

"How high can you jump?" Alex asked.

"High!" Cora said. And she jumped as high as she could.

"What grade are you in now? Six? Seven?"

"Nooo," Cora said, laughing. "I'm only in JK."

Alex looked to Paula for interpretation.

"Junior kindergarten," Paula said.

"Oh," Alex said, looking down at Cora. "We didn't have that when I was a kid. They just put us right into grade one."

Paula smiled at Cora and took her school bag from her.

"We better get inside, baby. It's getting cool out here. Can you say good-bye to Uncle Alex?"

"Bye, Uncle Alex."

"Hey, aren't you going to invite me in for a coffee?"

Paula looked at him, and then down the road where the school bus was turning onto another street.

"You're kidding, right?" she asked.

Alex didn't say anything; he just smiled.

"Carl's going to be home before long and—"

"Just a coffee," Alex said. "I haven't seen her in so long."

He smiled at Paula and messed up Cora's hair. Cora giggled.

"Okay. Sure."

Alex put his glasses back on and took Cora's hand.

"Lead the way, kid."

— • —

Alex and Paula sat at the kitchen table and drank their coffee in silence. Cora was pretending to be a dog. She sat under the table and barked every time Alex reached down to pet her head. She'd then get quiet, nuzzle up to his leg and let out a little howl. She found it tremendously funny and soon rolled onto her back and just giggled and waved her hands and kicked her feet in the air.

Alex watched her and then looked up at Paula.

"She's a happy kid," he said.

"Yes she is," Paula said. "And bright, too."

"She must get that from me."

Paula laughed and got up from the table. She walked to the cupboard and got out a bag of cookies.

"Do you remember the last time we saw each other?" Alex asked.

Paula looked at Alex and then down at Cora. She handed a cookie to Cora and then sat down, placing the bag on the table between her and Alex.

"Yes. And I don't think we need reminding," Paula said, nodding towards Cora.

"Oh, so you do remember?" Alex took a cookie out of the bag.

Cora got up and climbed on to her mother's lap.

"Remember what?" she asked, taking a bite from her cookie.

"Nothing, baby."

"The last time you saw me. Do you remember? We played tag, and I ran around the apartment playing your tin drum. And then you chased me right into the bathroom and I jumped into the tub with all my clothes on. Remember? It was full of water 'cuz you had just had a bath."

"Yeah. And you broke my tin drum," Cora yelled excitedly.

"And nearly broke my leg. You really remember that?"

"Yeah," Cora said. "I cried 'cuz you broke my drum, but you said you'd get me a new one. And then you did."

Cora looked up at Paula and smiled.

"I'll go get it," she said and jumped off her mother's lap.

Once Cora was out of the room, Alex leaned in close and looked slyly at Paula.

"Do you remember what else happened that night?" he asked.

"No," Paula said firmly. She tried to change the subject. "What did you say you were doing back in town?"

She picked up her mug and crossed the room to the window. The sun was already low in the western sky, floating somewhere just above the horizon. The air outside was cool. There was the smell of winter coming nearer. Before long the streets would be covered with snow and ice, and she and Carl would be married. She brought the coffee cup to her lips and watched as a car slowly drove by outside.

Alex walked over to where Paula stood.

"I didn't say. Shall I refresh your memory? About that night, I mean."

"No. That's not necessary." Paula didn't turn to face him but continued to look out the window.

"No? Let me try. My clothes got all wet in the tub so we had to throw them in the dryer. Then you got Cora to bed and we had a little drink. Right?"

"Yes."

"And we talked just like old times. Sitting on the couch with the TV on and the sound turned down. There was some music playing...Smokey Robinson, I think. And after a while, I kissed you. And you kissed me.... And then we made love."

"And then, in the morning, you left." Paula turned around to face Alex.

"I had somewhere to be."

"For a whole year?"

"I got tied up."

"It was a mistake to begin with, letting that happen. It was all a mistake. Except for Cora."

"Did you ever tell Carl about that night?" he asked.

"No," she said.

"It would be a shame if he found out."

"What are you suggesting, Alex?" Paula looked at him angrily.

"Nothing. I'm sorry. I didn't mean it like that. But sometimes I wish it wasn't over between us. You and me. Old times...."

Paula emptied her cup and rinsed it out in the sink. She stood there for a moment, brushed the hair from her forehead.

"Why couldn't you sit still for just a second, Alex? Why did you always have to run onto the next thing?"

"That's all over. I'm done with that. Finished moving around."

Alex took her hand in his. She let him hold it like that for a second but then pulled away.

"I see your timing's as good as ever. I think you should go—"

"I love you," Alex said, reaching for Paula's hand again. He leaned forward, and brought his lips to hers. She didn't push him away, not just then.

Cora ran down the hall and into the kitchen banging on her tin drum. Paula pulled away from Alex and sat down at the table. She wiped at something invisible on her lips.

"Can't find the drumsticks," Cora said, and whacked the drum loudly with her hands.

"But you found the drum," Alex said, still looking at Paula.

"Yep."

Paula knelt down next to Cora and tapped lightly on the drum with her fingers.

"Maybe we'll find them after Uncle Alex leaves. I think I know where they might be."

Cora looked up at Alex.

"Uncle Alex," she said.

"Yeah?"

"Don't break this one, okay?"

"Okay. I promise I won't."

"You can play it. Just don't break it."

Cora did a drum roll and marched off, singing a made-up song about dogs and ponies. Alex walked over to Paula and stroked her hair. She stood up.

"Quite a memory," he said.

"She gets that from you. Listen, you should go," Paula said. "You should really go."

"Things change, eh?"

Paula took a deep breath and looked at him.

"Yes, some things do."

"I'm moving back to town," Alex said. "Time to settle down, get a steady job, start a family." He smiled unevenly.

"You had a family," Paula said.

"I know...." He reached towards her.

"You're a fine piece of work, you know that?"

Paula shook her head and turned away from him.

"I'm different now. Everything is different now," he said.

"You're right, everything *is* different now. I'm different, too. And remember Carl? Well, he's also different. You can't just come back like this. It has to end. I haven't seen you in a year. And before that, you weren't around too much either. She doesn't even know you're her father, Alex."

"Who does she think her father is? Carl?"

"Well, what do you think? At least she sees him everyday."

Alex was quiet. He finished his coffee and put the mug on the counter.

"She should know who her father is."

"She should know, you're right. And should she also know that her father has missed every birthday? That he messed around when he should have been home with us? That he didn't seem to want very much to be a father? Why did you come back here, Alex? What do you want?"

"Another chance."

"I gave you another chance. And you took off."

"So that's it. You're just going to give up."

"No. You're the one who gave up."

Alex worked his jaw from side to side, thinking. Paula shook her head.

"Carl will be back soon. And as much as I'd love for you two to talk about the old days, I somehow think now is not the time."

"Yeah. Sure."

"I loved you, Alex. But I don't trust you. You can't expect me to drop everything and take you back just like that. Not after everything we've been through. I'm starting to get settled here. I'm getting my life sorted out."

He didn't say anything. And after a moment, Paula laughed. She punched him lightly on the shoulder. And eventually, he laughed, too.

"I've got some making up to do, then," he said.

"You've got something to do."

"You still love me?"

"You better go."

— • —

They slowly made their way down the hall. Cora came out of her room and marched down the hall ahead of them. She hit the drum rhythmically, leading the way to the door.

"Say good-bye to Uncle Alex, Cora. He has to go now."

Alex knelt down and gave her a hug. He looked up at Paula as he held on to her.

"Good to see ya, kid."

"Bye."

Cora grinned and broke free of his hug.

"You didn't fall in the tub this time," she said.

"No. I didn't, did I?"

Alex smiled at her and stood up.

"Well?" Paula said.

"Take care of her," he said. "And take care of yourself, too."

"I will."

"Maybe I'll see you around some time."

"Yeah."

Alex gave Paula a hug. And she hugged him back. He whispered in her ear.

"I think about you sometimes. At night. When I'm alone. I miss you then."

"I think about you, too. Sometimes. When I'm scrubbing the floor."

Paula laughed quietly and pushed him away. She straightened his collar and held out her hand.

"Good-bye," she said.

They shook hands, and Alex gave her a quick kiss on the lips. Paula stood at the door and watched him leave. He danced a little jig on the street and turned once to smile at her. He had on his fake glasses again.

"Can I ever change your mind?" he asked.

She smiled but shook her head no. And then she shooed him away with her hand, the way you would a dog that has been following you home.

"Go," she said. "Good-bye."

He waved one last time and then walked down the street and away. She watched and waited to see if he'd turn again, but he didn't, and soon he was out of sight.

And when she was sure he was gone, she closed the door and went back inside. Cora was sitting on the couch watching TV. She smiled up at her mother and patted the empty space beside her. Paula sat down and looked out the window. She expected a knock at the door, expected him to say he forgot his hat, or his wallet: an old trick of his like the salesman who puts his foot in the door so you can't close it. But no, he wouldn't be returning anytime soon. And if anyone were to knock at the door, it would likely be the trick-or-treaters. They came out so early now, not like when she was a kid. Carl would take Cora out when he got home from work. He really was a wonderful man, so full of love for them both. Paula thought about turning off the outside lights after they left and pretending no one was home when the trick-or-treaters came knocking. She would just sit in the kitchen with a coffee and a good book; she would enjoy the silence between knocks at the door. Maybe she'd start planning the wedding soon: nothing fancy, a few friends, a party. She'd tell Carl everything. It was time to move on.

"He's funny," Cora said, turning from the TV to face Paula.

Paula got up off the couch to go start dinner.

"Yes. He's funny, isn't he?" she said, but she was already thinking about something else.

— • —

Paula was standing at the door when Carl got home later that evening. He smiled when he saw her standing there and kissed her on the forehead.

"We need to talk," Paula said. "It's about us."

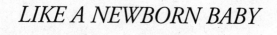

LIKE A NEWBORN BABY

Just before climbing into bed that night, Claire told Lou she had a secret to tell him—a confession—but it had to wait until after they made love. She smiled coyly and unclasped her bra, letting it fall to the floor. Lou didn't know what to think. With Claire, anything was possible. But seeing her standing there, naked and motioning with her index finger for him to join her under the covers, he decided to go ahead and jump in beside her.

They made love. Or had sex. Lou was too distracted to concentrate, and he found his mind wandering from one thing to the next. At one point, he thought about Claire's mother and half-expected the phone to ring—though there was no phone in his room. She had called like that one night just after Claire and he had made love in Claire's apartment. Lou reached over and picked up the phone before Claire could stop him. "*Coitus interruptus,*" he answered in his best Latin. Claire grabbed the phone from him and hung it up. Her mother called right back and said, "The strangest thing just happened." Claire laughed, said, "You don't say," not letting on that she was sharing her bed with someone.

Claire twisted her hip suddenly and Lou cringed. "Sorry," she said, smiling down at him. She blinked once before closing her eyes and continuing. Lou turned his attention to her hair. It was the color of hay, and it bounced and swished above him. It covered her face, and for a moment she looked to him like his dead sister, Joan. Had he been Catholic, he would have crossed himself and rushed to a confessional. But he wasn't Catholic, so he stayed put.

— • —

Lou remembered clearly the morning he visited Joan and first saw her bald head; he nearly cried. Joan made a joke of it, saying, "Better a bald head than no head." She was like that in the face of suffering. She shaved her head before the treatments had even started; she wanted to be in control of something. And she said that seemed like a good place to start: at the top. Her husband Tom shaved his head, too, in solidarity. Lou half-heartedly offered to shave his own head as well. But Joan said no, a bald head would only make him look like a creep. Lou was still standing in the doorway, looking down at his shoes.

After that, he didn't visit for a week or two. He made excuses, said he was busy, but the truth was he was afraid of breaking down and making a fool of himself when Joan—the one who was sick in the first place—was being so damn strong about it all.

— • —

Claire shuddered once, threw her head back, and groaned. Lou tried to smile, flare his nostrils, fan out his toes…but he only said, "Ahhh." And then he reached over and turned on the light.

"So," he said, "what is it you have to tell me?"

He searched for cigarettes and matches on the crowded milk crate he used as a bedside table. He found the pack under one of

Claire's magazines and pulled out two cigarettes. After lighting them both, he passed one to Claire.

Claire said, "I met another guy." She said, "He's just a year older than me. I think it's for the best, Lou. I mean, at your age, you could be my father." This last part wasn't exactly true, and she gave a little laugh through her nose.

Lou wasn't very surprised. He knew she would get bored sooner or later. She was young and easily distracted. And he was old, very old in her eyes: he was nearly thirty-eight. He asked Claire if anything had happened between her and this other guy, if they had been *together*—he said the word slowly so that she would understand the implication.

They were still laying in bed, the two of them. He had one arm under Claire's neck; it was becoming sore, and he tried to pull it out from under her. Claire turned and looked him in the eyes.

She said, "I was *with* him last night."

She's merciless, thought Lou, *and she doesn't even know it.* He nodded his head slowly and bit his lower lip as he considered what she had said.

"Last night," he said. "Get out of here. And take your stuff. I never want to see you again."

Lou kicked her out of his bed, and out of his life—that was how he saw things, anyway. If there was one thing he couldn't stand, it was a brazen cheater.

"I won't miss you that much," he told her as she gathered her things and dressed. He sat on the edge of the bed, naked, smoking another cigarette. Before she left, Lou asked, "Why would you do that? Why would you wait until after we made love to tell me such a thing."

"Because I knew it would be the last time," she said. "I loved you, Lou. But it just wouldn't work out between us. You've said so yourself."

Lou had said that, but he resented her reminding him of it now.

"Tramp," he said, quietly. "Slut."

Claire stopped pulling on her boots long enough to give him a look. She then stood up and turned to go.

"You're a bitch, Claire. A stuck-up, self-centered bitch."

"Fuck you, Lou," she whispered. She knew how thin the walls were.

"No. I've wanted to say that for a long time. You're a snob. You think you're too good for me, is that it? Think you're hot shit. Am I right?"

"Good-bye, Lou." She was headed for the door.

"Afraid to answer because you know it's true? I can take it. I'm not afraid to hear the truth—the way you are."

Claire spun around to face him.

"You know what? You're absolutely right. I am too good for you. You're a pathetic piece of shit."

She then turned her back on him and buttoned up her coat. Lou stood up and crossed the room.

"Get out," he said, pushing her towards the door.

Claire tripped on Lou's jeans which were still laying on the floor where he had left them. She landed on her knees and let out a stifled moan. Lou stood behind her, watching and waiting, mute. After a minute, she stood up slowly, rubbing her knees and brushing herself off.

"Ahh, shit. I'm sorry, Claire. Jesus, I didn't mean for that to happen. It's only—"

But Claire walked out, slamming the door behind her.

— • —

Alone in his room afterwards, Lou got out his old trumpet and dusted it off. It had been ages since he last played it. He bought the horn at a pawn shop almost seventeen years ago, at a time when he had a job and some extra money. It cost nearly two hundred dollars. Lou didn't know if he was getting ripped off or not—but he didn't really care. He just wanted the horn, to play it, and to feel the cool metal in his hands. And when he finally brought it home that day, he was not unlike his sister bringing home her newborn baby from the hospital: he handled it so gently, feeling the weight of it in his hands, and then he laid it out on his bed and stared at it. It was an hour or more before he would bring the horn to his lips and play it for the first time.

Or try to play, at any rate. He was a terrible trumpet player and only chose that instrument in a high school music class because it had just three valves. That was when people started calling him Lou or Louis; it was meant sarcastically because he had no sense of melody at all. But he was dedicated to the trumpet and carried it with him everywhere he went. His real name was Colin. But the name Lou stuck, and now he used Lou exclusively, though he never had it legally changed. Even his own mother called him Lou. And as bad a trumpet player as he was, Lou persisted all these years, playing now and then without ever really improving. He found himself picking up the horn when he needed to think, or when something was troubling him. Sometimes he put the horn down for months at a time. But then he'd pick it up again, dust it off, and play a few notes until someone banged on the wall or floor or ceiling to make him stop. He lived in a rooming house with some other lost souls, as he called them—it was a phrase his grandmother had used—they were mostly men, adrift in the world, searching for something they couldn't name.

Naked, and holding the trumpet in his hands, Lou sat on his bed wondering what it was Claire saw in him in the first place. He was an older man with no job and no money, and he lived in a rooming house. Perhaps she saw the man he had been, or would be if things just worked out for him once in a while. Maybe—this thought had crossed his mind more than once—maybe she saw him as a charity case; maybe she felt sorry for him the way most people did after his breakdown, after Joan died. Whatever it had been, it lasted for nearly a year, more or less, which was a significant period of time for Lou to be with a woman.

— • —

Before Joan's health got worse, it got better. And Lou started visiting her at home when Tom and the kids were out at work and school. It was Tom's idea. Tom was worried about Joan during the day when she was alone. ("All that time to herself," he said, "can't be good for her.") Joan wasn't well enough to go back to teaching, which is what she did before she got sick, and they couldn't afford to have a nurse stay and look after her. Not that she needed looking after, she told Lou. Since Lou didn't have a job, and since he had nothing else to do, Tom asked him if he could visit with Joan and help her with anything she needed.

Lou liked the regularity of it. He got there every morning at around ten or so. And when the kids got home, they'd make supper together and Lou would stay until all the dishes were done. On his way home, he'd stop for a drink at a bar where he would sometimes stay until late evening. He had his own problems that Joan helped him forget about during the day, and at night he did whatever else he could do to forget.

He had started smoking a lot of dope and doing the occasional line of coke, and that was getting expensive. He owed people money. And not having a job didn't help matters. But Joan was there and she was happy to listen to his problems. "If you can call them problems," she said. It helped her to forget about her own troubles for a while. There were days they would sit in silence, drinking herbal tea and maybe watching—or staring at—the TV. Lou would get uncomfortable with the silence at times, and he'd start to say something but then change his mind. Mostly, he was happy to sit there with Joan, listening to her talk about whatever was on her mind. He had even convinced her to smoke some pot with him. "It's therapeutic," he told her.

Some afternoons they'd sit and talk about their childhood. It amazed them both how different their memories were. Joan remembered it fondly—recalling long, hot summer days of lolling about in the backyard or staying up late with her brothers to watch slasher movies or Colombo. The years were filled with gaps, things she didn't remember at all. Lou remembered only the tragic events, the bad times, and when it came to these memories, he remembered them clearly, describing to Joan details she couldn't possibly recall.

"Do you remember when dad left that last time?" Lou asked one afternoon.

She did not. Not clearly. Their father was a large man who was away on business half the year. He barely knew his children and they barely knew him. And that's the way it would always be. Before leaving for another trip that would last a month or more, their father would play a game of peek-a-boo at the door; he did this even when they were all too old to find the game amusing. He'd pretend to leave, then poke his head back in the door—"I'm not gone yet!"—and then pretend to leave again. It would sometimes go on for twenty minutes. And after a while, they couldn't help but laugh.

"Then one day," Lou told Joan, "he did it just like that: poking his head in and out to the point of embarrassment. We finally asked him to just go. And he did. And he never came back."

They were both quiet for a moment. Joan took a sip from her tea cup.

"Thanks for raising my spirits," she told him. "You realise that's the whole point of you being here, right? To make me feel better. Tom was afraid he'd come home some day and find me in the garage with the doors closed and the car running. You know, the headline would read, 'Lonely housewife, stricken with cancer, ends own life by carbon monoxide poisoning.' Puh-leeze."

They both chuckled. And then they couldn't stop. They laughed until tears rolled down their faces and their whole bodies shook. Lou even fell off his chair. When they were finally done, and the tears were wiped from their eyes, and the last little "ha" finally escaped—sounding like not much more than a breath of air—Joan looked down at Lou.

"We're sick, Lou. We're sick, sick bastards laughing about something like that."

And then they laughed some more.

— • —

As Lou sat alone in his room, the smell of Claire still close by, he suddenly felt that his love for her was more real than ever before. There had been times when he couldn't see Claire in his future; it was like staring into a crystal ball and seeing only his own reflection surrounded by a milky void, alone with himself. And he had always thought about—and watched—other women, older women. But he was like that. With Joan gone, Lou knew he needed a woman in his life, someone to keep him on track the way she had done, or attempted to. Now that Claire was gone, too, he found himself worrying that she had been the one who was supposed to fill that void, the one he was intended to marry: his soulmate. And he let her slip through his fingers.

Suddenly, he could only remember the good times.

Things had been going well, he thought. He bought her little gifts whenever he could afford to. Some trinket he picked up somewhere, or once, a bottle of expensive perfume he bought from a guy in a bar. He wasn't embarrassed that Claire always had more money than him. And that she usually paid the way for both of them when they went out. He was a little old fashioned, but he got used to things being the way they were. Claire never hesitated to buy him groceries, or even clothes every now and then; and she lent him money whenever he needed it—he didn't even have to ask most times. He knew that behind his back his friends joked about him being a kept man, a gigolo to a younger woman. But Claire was just generous and kind to Lou, and not once did she mention the money he owed, or the gray hairs on his head, or even the small stray hairs that were beginning to poke out of his nose and ears. What had happened to change all that? Where had he gone wrong?

Lou played the trumpet until his lungs ached and his lips became numb. He ignored the neighbours pounding on his locked door. And he ignored their insults. But after a while, one distinct voice rose above the rest, a low, raspy voice that said, "Go get her, you crazy love sick fool. Tell her you're sorry. And bring that blasted horn with you."

The walls *were* thin.

The voice belonged to Norman, the old man who stayed in the room next to Lou's. He had imposed himself on Lou since the day Lou moved in; he acted like a surrogate father or a big brother, and he made Lou's business his business. It was Norman who gave Lou the thumbs up when Claire started coming around. (That first Christmas, Norman slipped an old wrinkled five dollar bill into Lou's hand and told him to go buy a bottle of wine for himself and his girl.) He'd tell Lou all the good places to get free food, and he made sure Lou took his medication every day—if Lou got worked up over anything, he'd lose control, black out. But Norman made sure that didn't happen while he was around. He knew about these things, he said. He said he had been through a war.

Lou put the horn down and got dressed. He unlocked his door and saw Norman standing in the hall, smoking a hand-rolled ciga-rette. Norman was short with a stocky build. He had thick, round fingers stained yellow from smoking as much as he did. His teeth were stained brown and yellow. And his hair, the same dirty color but slick and wet looking, reflected the overhead light in the hall-way.

"Hi, Norman."

"You know, Bix Beiderbecke was just sixteen when he first heard Armstrong playing on a river boat? Armstrong himself was only eighteen at the time. That's when Bix went out and got a horn of his own. Sixteen. Imagine that."

"What's your point, Norman?"

"Just that it's never too late," he said, with no apparent logic. "Listen, I don't know what just happened in here, but you gotta go tell her you're sorry. You're playing that thing for her—not for us— and she can't even hear it. Go find her. Play outside her window if you have to. You won't have to say anything at first. She'll under-stand."

"You really think so?"

"Sure. Trust me. I have some perspective on matters of the heart. After all, I was married for twenty-seven years. Did I ever tell you about that?"

"No. What happened?"

Norman leaned against the door frame and pulled another cigarette out of his shirt pocket. He lit it off the cigarette he had been smoking and then dropped the finished one to the floor and stepped on it.

"She died. Or left me. Or both," Norman said, taking his time. "It was a long time ago. Just get out of here, kid. I saved your life. Some of these guys here are not so refined as us, not so interested in the subtleties of jazz the way we are. They wanted to tear your door down and drag you and that horn outside."

"One minute everything was fine and then...."

"I know, I know. Sometimes there's just no explaining. If I live to be a hundred years old, I'll never understand women. Just go over there and say you're sorry. That's a start."

"But I'm not sure I am. I mean, she's the one—"

"Do you want her back?"

"Yeah, I think so."

"Then get out of here and tell her you're sorry."

— • —

Lou went into his room and thought about what Norman had said. He did want things to be as they were, and he was willing to say he was sorry and to forget about what had happened. He slipped on a thin jacket and grabbed his trumpet. Once outside, he felt happier, somehow lighter and freer—like an actor in a movie about to do something that will change the course of his life. He walked and ran the twenty or so blocks to Claire's apartment. He tried to imagine what her reaction might be. She'd be so surprised: he'd never played for her before. He was sure no one had. She'd have to forgive him, take him back. And he'd forgive her, too. And then everything would be fine. He would ask her to marry him. She would say yes.

As he thought of this, and of his sister, who was always on his mind, he felt his heart beating under his coat. Thumpthump. Thumpthump. Thumpthump. And it reminded him of a train rolling down the tracks, over a bridge, through the hills and away. It felt good to be alive.

— • —

The headlights of passing cars cut lazily through the falling snow in front of Claire's apartment. Lou stood across the street and looked up at her window. It was lit up, but he couldn't see anyone inside. He stretched his fingers and cracked his knuckles. If he was going to do this, he had to do it right. He took a deep breath, brought the trumpet to his lips and played a long, sad, minor note. He closed his eyes and tried to remember how to play some of those songs he had learned so long ago. He played what he imagined to be a lovely, soulful tune; perhaps something he had once heard while listening to records in Norman's room. The uneven notes filled the air, mingling with the snowflakes. He opened his eyes, still playing, and waited for Claire to appear in the window.

It wasn't long before someone came to the window. But it wasn't Claire. It was one of her roommates. She looked down at Lou and shook her head. Then Claire came to the window and yelled down at him.

"Get out of here," she said.

He kept playing. Someone else opened a window behind him.

"Shut that thing up," a man's voice said.

Lou continued to play.

Claire and her roommate watched for a minute and then closed the window and pulled the curtains together. Lou stopped to catch his breath. He decided to try something a little more up-beat, a little jazzier. He brought the horn to his lips a second time and began playing what he imagined as an up-tempo tune.

After a few more minutes, Claire opened the window again. Lou stopped playing.

"I'm sorry," he yelled up at her.

"Get out of here, Lou. Go home."

"I'm playing for you, Claire. I love you."

"Good-bye, Lou."

"But Claire, don't you see—"

"Go."

Lou's arms dropped to his sides. Something occurred to him.

"Is he there?"

"Who?"

"Him. The guy. The younger guy?"

"No, Lou. He's not here."

"Good."

He started playing again. He was going to play until she came down there and talked to him. Until she forgave him and fell into his arms. And that stuff about the other guy, he could easily forget about that. But she closed the window again and then turned out the light. Lou played. A voice from behind told him to shut up. But he just played.

Claire's roommate appeared at the window again.

"I'm going to call the cops if you don't get out of here," she yelled down at him. "I mean it."

Snow kept falling and Lou kept playing. He thought he must look like quite a sight from up there, almost magical in that light, with the snow flakes falling all around him. He thought about Louis Armstrong on a riverboat down south, and Bix seeing him for the first time. He thought it might be like that for Claire. Look at me, he wanted to say, listen to what I have to tell you. But instead, he played.

"I mean it," the roommate said again.

Lou stopped.

"Get Claire," he shouted.

Claire came to the window.

"What?"

He softened up a little.

"It's a beautiful night out here," he said. "With the snow and everything."

"Sandra's going to call the cops, Lou."

"I love you, Claire. Doesn't that mean anything to you?"

"Lou, please...."

"I want you back. I don't want this to happen to us. Come on. Just come down here and talk to me, please."

"No. I have nothing to say to you."

"I mean it. Come down or I'll keep playing." He held the trumpet threateningly close to his lips. "Come down here or I'll start up again."

"Sandra will call the cops if you don't go home, Lou."

"Remember that you started this, Claire. So fuck you."

He blasted a loud, discordant note. And then kept blasting it again and again with increasing speed and volume. The man in the window behind Lou was furiously shouting for him to stop. A few lights went on in Claire's building. Faces appeared in the windows. Lou's face turned red, then purple. His cheeks and eyes were bulging. He held the last note for as long as he could, and then he collapsed to the ground. The trumpet fell out of his hands and into the street.

He remained motionless on the sidewalk, watching the snow flakes hit the ground and vanish. One by one, the little flakes disappeared as they fell upon the wet pavement. He thought he could hear them hissing as they evaporated all around him. He sat up and held his head in his hands and began to weep.

— • —

It happened when Lou got the job at the gas station; Joan's health took another turn—this time for the worse. The new job meant that Lou couldn't spend as much time with her anymore, but he went over when he could, spent mornings there when he worked the night shift. It was Lou who first noticed when Joan's health turned. She slipped one morning while walking from the kitchen into the living room. She was carrying a plastic bowl filled with grapes. The fall wasn't much, but Lou saw the look on her face as she tried to pick up the scattered grapes off the floor. Tears came to her eyes, and she quickly wiped them away. Lou had to help her to her feet and then over to the couch. She said she needed to rest, that she was fine, just tired. But even then, she looked scared.

She ended up back in the hospital. The doctors talked about sending her to Toronto, but Joan wouldn't go, and the doctors didn't put up much of a fight about it. She said she knew it would be of no use. She was tired of being a guinea pig, tired of waiting to die. And she wanted to be close to her family. Lou went to visit though he hated hospitals, hated the colour of the walls, the nurses rushing past and that smell, like medicine and disease. But he sat by her bed and talked with her while Tom waited out in the hall. She had said she wanted to be alone with Lou for a minute.

She was pale and ghostly thin that night. Her face had a sickly green pallor to it. And she was weak, too. She found it difficult to speak for even short periods of time. Lou occasionally wiped her brow with a cool damp cloth and held a glass of water to her lips so she could take small sips. She rambled on and would then stop mid-sentence and close her eyes as if having fallen asleep. But then, after a short rest, she'd start up again. The nurse warned Lou when he arrived that because of the medication Joan was on, she would not be entirely lucid.

Joan opened her eyes and saw Lou looking at his watch. She smiled.

186 • *People Leaving*

"Going some place?" she asked. "Listen, Lou, I want you to smarten up. Go find yourself a nice girl and settle down. Stay out of trouble, because I'm not always going to be around to catch you when you fall."

"Yes you will," he said.

"And Lou," Joan said, closing her eyes after a moment. "If anything happens to Tom after I'm gone, I want you to take care of the kids. Even though you don't have a wife or even a good job or much of anything at all," she tried to laugh but only coughed, "I know that if you had to, you could provide a good home for them. There'd be money left for you, so you wouldn't have to worry about that. They love you so much." She had begun to cry.

He fought back tears until it became too much, so he let them fall. He didn't know what to say.

Joan opened her eyes and said, "Don't say anything. I know you'll do it if you have to. But let's hope you never have to."

Then she closed her eyes to rest.

That night, in Joan's room, Lou gave her a hug before leaving. He worried that if he squeezed too tight, he'd hurt her frail body, and so he was very gentle. He could feel her bones through her hospital gown and after all that talking, she hardly had the strength to hug him back. Lou wanted to pick her up then and carry her outside to see the stars and the moon—or to drive off with her and find someone who could make her well again. But instead, all he said was, "Good night." And he walked down the sickeningly white corridor to the elevator.

She died a few weeks later.

And it happened like that: in a flash. In no time at all, it seemed, she was gone forever. The funeral was a blur. Lou showed up drunk, but no one said anything. He got up to say a few words but ended up leaning with his head on the casket, sobbing. His older brother had to pull him away, help him back to his seat. He left as soon as it was over, stopping at the door only long enough to shake Tom's hand. He tried to tell him how sorry he was but couldn't find the words.

"It's not easy for any of us," Tom said.

A few mornings after the funeral, Lou's mother stopped in to check up on him. She was worried because he wasn't answering her calls, and he hadn't shown up for work. Lou was badly hung-over and unshaven when he answered the door. He was in his underwear.

"What the hell are you doing? You're a mess," his mother said.

"Mind your own business," Lou said.

"Clean yourself up. How do you think she'd feel if she saw you like this?"

"She won't see me like this."

— • —

Lou started thinking about leaving town after Joan's death. He figured that he could afford to drive to Toronto, maybe. Once there, he could sell the car and find himself a job. It wasn't much of a plan but it was all he had. He started thinking about it all the time. That's when he stole the money from the gas station he was working at. As a goodwill gesture, he left behind enough cash for the float the following day—but he took everything else. As he counted the money that night, he became overwhelmed with the thought of being a fugitive, of being on the run. Of getting caught. And it was just too much. He imagined Joan like one of those angels in the cartoons, the angel sitting on your shoulder telling you to do the right thing.

The next morning, Lou showed up at the gas station with the money in a brown paper bag. He put it on his boss's desk and apologized. The boss fired him on the spot, of course, and made sure Lou wouldn't get a job at any other station in town. But he wouldn't press charges. He said, "You've got enough troubles. You've just gotta straighten yourself out. And going to jail would only make you worse."

Things only got worse after that. Lou rarely left his room, and he wouldn't talk to anyone. He looked terrible, was drunk most of the time and barely ate anything at all. He broke down slowly, bit by bit, until his mother convinced him to admit himself into a hospital. "To get straightened out," she said. And he did, but he was never the same, and he'd be the first to admit that.

— • —

"I'm nothing without you," Lou cried into the night. "I don't deserve to live."

He was sprawled on the sidewalk, staring up into the falling snow. He yelled at the top of his lungs, "I'm nothing. No one can love me. No one loves me." Then he closed his eyes and kicked his legs out wildly.

Claire ran out the front door of her building. She called from the other side of the street.

"Lou. Please stop it. You'll hurt yourself. Please, Lou. Before the police get here, just stop."

Lou didn't hear her. He continued to yell and kick.

— • —

The wet trumpet reflected the lights of the police van when it came to a stop. The headlights were trained on Lou, and two police officers got out and walked towards him. He was still laying on the ground, sobbing now as people watched from all around. Claire remained on the other side of the street with her hands covering her mouth. The officers approached Lou.

"Sir? Are you all right?"

They knelt down beside him and tried to calm him down. His screaming subsided but he continued to sob.

"Come on now. Let's get you up."

Together, the two police officers helped Lou to his feet.

"Have you been drinking tonight, sir?"

Claire ran over.

"He's not drunk. He's got something wrong with his...with his head." She pointed to her own head. "This has happened before. Not as bad as this but...."

Lou was breathing heavily. He couldn't focus on any of them standing there, and suddenly he went limp and fell back to the ground. And again started screaming.

The police officers told Claire they would have to take him away.

"No!" Lou yelled back at them. "No no no!"

The officers picked him up and dragged him to the van. Claire walked along side, trying to subdue him.

"Lou. Please just go with them. It'll be okay. I'll come down there, too. I'll be there when you get there. Please. Lou."

The officers pushed him into the van and closed the door.

Lou kicked his feet and banged his fists against the walls inside the van. One of the police officers knocked on the door with her night stick. She told Lou that he was only making things worse for himself. Lou turned and kicked at the doors. He could hear voices on the other side. The cops'. Claire's. He stopped kicking and was quiet for a moment.

"My trumpet," he called out.

"I've got it, Lou. It's okay. I've got it," Claire said.

"Claire...." He spoke with a shaky voice. But he didn't know what else to say.

He looked around and tried to catch his breath. There was a dim light above his head, and some light coming in from the other side of the caged window that looked into the front of the van. The air inside was cool against his face, not unpleasant. He sat up and tried to remember what had happened. Norman told him to go play a song for Claire. But what had he played? He thought for a moment, but he couldn't remember. It was colder now, and Lou rubbed his hands together. His pants were wet and his hair, too. He wrapped his arms around himself and tried to remain steady as the van pulled away from the curb and into traffic.

After a while, he sat back against the wall and closed his eyes. He imagined himself opening his trumpet case on a busy city street. He saw this as though watching it from above, like an out-of-body experience, vivid but dream-like. He carefully took out the trumpet, leaving the case open on the sidewalk before him. The sun was shining. The air was filled with the sound of traffic and humming engines, voices rising and falling, and the wind whistling past: it all began to sound like music. He stood tall and straight, and brought the gleaming trumpet to his lips. And then he just played and played while all around him people walked past, dropping loose change into the case, and smiling at Lou as the sad, beautiful music filled the space between himself and them.

HOW ART THOU FALLEN?

The year is 1962. A man sits at an outside café holding a glass of ice water to his sweaty brow. He gazes through the water and glass at the man sitting across the table from him. He is having dinner with an old lover whom he has not spoken to in many years. Leonard, the man with the ice water, says, "It has been so long since I have had a drink." And he says, "I am a bad man who has done bad things, but I still love you." He speaks like this while his ex-lover, Peter, looks on from the opposite side of the table, embarrassed and silent, nodding furtively to the waiter to bring the bill.

"We still live in an age," Leonard says ironically, "where we are punished most harshly not for our acts but for our secrets. Please forgive me my digressions in the past. You are looking at the new me."

Peter is still embarrassed and can't help but laugh. He has heard this so many times before—with slight variations every time. He looks on, not knowing how to respond. He thinks of other places he would rather be. His lover is waiting for him just three blocks away at a bar in an expensive hotel. He is a younger man, the new lover, handsome and bearded. While the man that sits across from him is older; his face is fleshy and porridge coloured.

Peter has been listening. But he is also thinking about that time, long ago. And how things have changed. There is no denying he once had feelings for this man. But now....

"Leonard," Peter says, "so much has changed. We have changed. I am not the same man I was then. And neither are you."

And this is true, Peter thinks. No matter how hard he tries—and he does try—he can't conjure up those old feelings—only disbelief and confusion. How, he thinks, did I ever love a man that had the potential to end up like this man before me? He scolds himself for having these thoughts. I am old now, too, he thinks. He scans Leonard's face for traces of the man he once was.

Leonard shakes his head sadly from side to side.

He, Leonard, really has let himself go, thinks Peter. There was the arrest, the suicide attempts, the drinking. He had fallen a long, long way. Peter blushes at a memory that slips into his head from that faraway place he thought was buried deep, and forgotten. The memory he has took place fourteen or fifteen years ago. They had just met days before and were in bed talking the morning after their first night together. Leonard got out of bed to look out the window. Peter said to him: "You look like an angel." Just that one sentence that now comes back to haunt him. No, not a haunting. It just comes back to him now. He remembers how Leonard was once angelic: his pale skin and soft blue eyes. The only other visible colour was on Leonard's face: his cheeks, red as though slapped or warm or both. His thin, light hair glowed with an ethereal light as he stood against the window that morning. He was boy-like in his beauty, though he was well past thirty at the time. He had an innocence then that lessened his years, made him appear not unlike an angel.

"How art thou fallen from heaven, O Lucifer, son of the morning?" Peter says the words aloud, then smiles, hopelessly.

Leonard places his water glass down on the table, stands and bows slightly before his old friend.

Peter looks up at Leonard's bowed head, his gray, thinning hair—dirty, too—and he feels, for the first time, sorry for the man. But there is nothing he can do. Or will do. And what will happen—mystery and not-mystery that it is; because, really, they all know what will happen to the poor man—will happen. He has been hiding out in his apartment for months, refusing most visitors. And what does he eat up there? He doesn't cook. He drinks, mostly, and orders in. The money is running out, and time is no longer a friend but an old, war-tired enemy.

Leonard opens his mouth to speak.

"Once upon a time, when I was just a boy, my mother asked me where I had been. I made something up and told her a lie. I can remember neither the lie nor the truth. But I remember the telling of the lie. The ease with which it slipped out of my mouth, between my lips like a cool slice of peach. I just opened up and: Ahhhhh. And I remember, too, what my mother said. She said: "Such a small boy and such a big sinner." I don't know how she knew I was lying. She just did. And so, I thought, that's it: I am a liar; I have sinned. But that was only the beginning. And I have told many lies since, I know. And they have added up and they tower over me now and teeter and will someday fall."

He stops here and sits back down. He rolls the glass of ice water slowly across his brow. The mostly thawed ice cubes make the faintest clinking sound as they hit the side of the glass. Leonard places the glass back down on the table without taking a sip. He continues to speak.

"You know, I was married to a woman for a while. Yes, it is funny. Laugh. I do…now. But then, then I didn't laugh. I swore I forgot how. You know, I never had fun after you left? No, it's true. Please…Peter."

Peter catches his breath. The way Leonard says his name has not changed. And there is in an instant this recognition—that soon passes.

"We lived in a small apartment near a river," Leonard is saying. "When the weather began to warm, the ice on the river melted—slowly at first but gaining momentum with each degree. At night, I could hear the ice crack and break away from the shore. Ice floes—surrounded by black water—would form and float down river, eventually breaking in two and then three. Soon, the smaller floes would thaw, crack and break in two, in three and then dissolve altogether until all that remained was the swollen river—water rushing past the shore, pushing away from the dark city to a place we couldn't see or follow. When there was still ice to walk on—dirty ice that seemed to breathe—children tested it with sticks and with cautious feet that soon became reckless, running on the frozen river, on a piece of ice the size of a typical skating rink. It would inevitably crack and split, break away from that ice anchored to the shore: leaving the children stranded—waving their childish arms at the small figures standing on the shore. Figures becoming smaller with every minute, every degree. The children would float down river standing on their uncertain raft, scared; their throats hoarse from calling for help. Waiting and wondering if help would arrive in time. And wondering, too, I'm sure—like all of us—wondering what lay ahead, down that dark expanse of river.

"And when there was still ice to walk on, thin dirty ice…my wife announced she was pregnant. That night—Are you listening, Peter?—That night I walked down to the river and stepped out onto a piece of ice no larger than this table here. I lay on my back and floated peacefully down river, watching the stars above and thinking about nothing much at all. When I awoke, my skin was blue, and I wished I had gills. It seems some men had fished me out and saved—Do you understand?—saved my life. They gave me a second chance which I had tried to squander away, or lose in a poker game."

Peter watches Leonard's face, trying to guess at the emotion hidden there.

"What about your wife?" he asks. "The baby?"

"She lost it."

"Why are you telling me this now?" Peter asks.

But Leonard is carried off by his own thoughts that have strayed beyond this hot afternoon and this café with his old, long since lost lover. He is no longer with him but, perhaps, out on the river, stranded on the ice, counting the stars overhead.

"I will now take your leave," Leonard says. "I'll bother you no more." His chair scrapes against the pavement as he stands. "I just wanted to see you this last time. You see, I am very ill. It happens like that, you know. The thing that gets you in the end is not the thing you always suspected. Not the thing you avoided all your life with a false sense of premonition. But it is the thing, the awful, damaging, painful thing that has been growing inside of you all along. Quietly building itself while you sleep, while you eat, while you make love...."

Peter remains quiet, looking into Leonard's dark, tired eyes.

"But I am more hopeful," Leonard says. "More optimistic than ever before. Of course, that's not saying much, now is it?"

Peter tries to smile.

Leonard reaches into his pocket for his wallet but Peter waves his hand away.

"I've got it," Peter says and produces his own thick wallet. He lets a few bills drop on to the table, and then he stands up.

Leonard bows once more, looks up with one last imploring— but ultimately hopeless—look and then walks away.

Peter is weary, his arms hang limply at his side. He looks, if one were to walk by and glance at him briefly, like a marionette with so many loose strings hanging. He considers calling after Leonard, but he doesn't know what he would say. So he just stands where he is, puts his hands in his pockets, and watches Leonard slump away. And before long Leonard turns a corner and is out of sight. And then the feeling passes. Peter straightens his tie, brushes back the hair from his eyes and walks away.

— • —

When Peter arrives at the bar, his lover gets up from his chair and greets him. Peter sits down before speaking and orders a drink simply by pointing to what his lover is drinking and nodding his head to the server. He takes a long sip from his glass and begins speaking.

"A man sits at an outside café holding a glass of ice water to his sweaty brow. He gazes through the water and glass...."

But Peter keeps a secret of the memory that flashed before him—Leonard and he together so many years ago. He keeps a secret, too, of the image of Leonard naked against the window, his hair a halo above his head, his thin, pale body exquisite in the morning light. And walking home with his lover afterwards, Peter rolls this secret around like a peach pit in his mouth, testing the sad grooves with his tongue. Sad the way rain can be sad when you happen to be feeling that way.

Somewhere across town, the buds of angel wings are sprouting on Leonard's back.